Bruce Whitehead has worked in the Computer Software industry for 50 years. He started as a mainframe computer programmer back in the 60's and progressed through the ranks from systems analyst to subject matter expert, and then Project Manager. He owned and operated his own software consulting firm for almost ten years. Bruce is currently a Senior Project Manager for a leading HealthCare service provider. He lives with his wife Jane and their grandson Jake, in Tallahassee, Florida.

Bruce Whitehead

IF IT TAKES A LIFETIME

To Emily!
Thanks for your
support and excellent
service!

Br[ ]Whitehead

AUSTIN MACAULEY PUBLISHERS™

London • Cambridge • New York • Sharjah

Ordering Information:
Quantity sales: special discounts are available on quantity purchases by corporations, associations, and others. For details, contact the publisher at the address below.

Publisher's Cataloguing-in-Publication data
Whitehead Bruce.
If It Takes a Lifetime

ISBN 9781641820325 (Paperback)
ISBN 9781641820349 (Hardback)
ISBN 9781641820332 (E-Book)

The main category of the book — Fiction/Fantasy/General

www.austinmacauley.com

First Published (2018)
Austin Macauley Publishers Ltd™
40 Wall Street, 28th Floor
New York, NY 10005
USA

mail-usa@austinmacauley.com
+1 (646) 5125767

The Castle

It is almost midnight as I quietly creep down the cold and cramped corridor, I quickly come to recognize this place... if not this time. This is the old Bentley Castle... but when is it? I am certain I will find out shortly... if I live long enough to calculate the current space-time reference (*STR*).

Seeing only subtle light coming from the staircase ahead, I must make the decision... to go up or to go down. While I've made this decision many times in the past... and many times in the future, the path I take on each trip is always distinctly different. And of course, that is because the time-space reference is constantly changing. In objective time, at least, I've been on this trek through space and time for at least ten years. In subjective time, I've covered, if my calculations are correct, several dozen centuries.

No time to reflect or contemplate now... it is once again... survival time. If I can make it out of this monstrous maze without dying... then I have a slim chance of surviving in whatever *STR* I find myself once I am able to leave this castle behind and head into the *City*.

On this day, I decide to go *up* and quickly note that to my audio-log, which is recording everything... and has been since I began this unfortunate journey in 2049. I usually alternate between up and down, but sometimes one feels right or one feels wrong. I have learned, over these years, to trust my instincts... although that has led me into quite a few disastrous situations. But then, even the good journeys usually end up as disasters... if I remain long enough in a single *STR*.

As I creep up the solitary confinement of the stairway, I begin looking for the *Entities.* They can arrive from almost anywhere or sometimes even nowhere. They are not always waiting for me to arrive but, especially if my path becomes too predictable, they know I'm coming and usually have a plan to take me out before I am able to get out of the castle and get to the relatively safe haven of the *City*.

As is customary, but not mandatory, the lights dim as I begin ascending the staircase. I remain constantly on alert. I activate torch-mode on my *SmartComm*. Even with only half of the LCDs remaining active, I can see, perhaps, ten feet ahead… and that is enough. Finally, I reach the top of the spiraling staircase… I never stop on the in-between floors. It is either all the way to the top… or all the way to the bottom floor… the often damp and always dingy prison dungeon. Twice, when I decided to investigate those middle level floors… but I choose not to relive those experiences… as I am already frightened enough.

This path looks encouraging. Once I arrive at the top floor and exit the stairway (never looking back), I see light ahead, and deactivate torch-mode. Best not to draw any unwanted attention. I am back into creep mode, looking left, right, and above. They never come from below… something about solid floors they don't like… if I can ever figure that out… but no time to think about that now.

I arrive in the main ballroom. The number of cobwebs and the state of the lighting system lead me to believe I am now in the mid to late 1800s. I'll confirm later… if I remain alive.

I slowly and cautiously walk through the ballroom and am almost out into the courtyard when they jump. It's the open spaces 'in between' that usually get me. If I can make it to the light, I'm usually safe… but not tonight… not at midnight.

This time there are seven of them. Three red-eyed, monstrous-looking, winged creatures, and the four black phantoms, maybe soft-clones… it's hard to tell in this dimly lit hallway. I decide to make a run for the door… if I can make it to the courtyard, then at least I have a fighting chance… but the first red-eyed entity grabs me, I'm on the ground and almost instantly the others arrive, teeth flaring, voices roaring… shrieking… and begin… consuming me. Even though I've been through this horror many times, I can still hear myself screaming as my bones begin to break, and I both hear and feel the flesh being torn from my already bleeding and battered body, as I am slowly and quite painfully devoured.

Part 1
Living the Virtual Life

Reset and Restart

I awake in a field. No castle in sight... that is certainly good news. As I get up from the ground, I notice a painful kink in my neck. I'm not getting old, but if I am aging inside this *Sim*, then I am now in my early thirties, and since life has not been all that good to me as of late, I am beginning to feel my age. I guess... being eaten alive hundreds of times will tend to age a person... but I am only assuming.

As I walk toward the distant ridge, I notice a round sun, redder than usual, and a bit smaller than normal. It is warm... maybe 75, so I am content, for the moment. As I look around, I notice the land surrounding me is mostly barren. No trees, no vegetation, and hopefully, no animal, monsters, or mechanical life... but it is much too early to tell what my near future may hold.

I walk toward the sun for almost half a day. I am traveling on a slight incline, and I seem to be getting no closer to the edge of the ridge than I was an hour ago. I stop, rest, there is no water, no food... but for this day... I am okay.

I continue my trek; the sun is just about at midday... still no sign of life... but I now appear to be getting closer to the ridge. My calves are beginning to ache, I can tell I am walking uphill... so must stop frequently, stretch my legs, relax, and just sit.

By early afternoon, I detect a slight change in scenery. There are small patches of grass, the rocks are larger, and I spot a few cactus-like plants, sporadically placed here and there.

I arrive at the edge of the ridge rather abruptly. I look over... I am possibly a thousand feet above the basin below. I see a stream... a small river actually, given this height, and I notice the *City*… way off in the distance… possibly twenty miles… or more.

I begin searching for a way down but don't spot one. That, in itself, is unusual, since I always program a way out of the trap and into the *City*. What good would the *Game* be if there was no way to get into the meat of it… no pun intended?

As I study the landscape below and scan the edge of the cliff, looking for a path or any kind, I hear a noise behind me. I turn and there they are.

I count fourteen *Gondolas*… all exactly eight feet high, almost square, looking like they are direct descendants from that ole *Minecraft* game… which of course, they are.

I try to remember my last encounter with *Gondolas*, maybe I can reason with them. I move toward them… a few steps, and they begin to form a circle. "I am not looking for trouble," I state. "I just need help… getting to that *City*… see over there," I point.

One of the *Gondolas* approaches. "We are not authorized to allow you to pass. You must turn back, retreat down this mountain, and proceed in another direction."

"No," I state, "I must continue toward the *City*… that is my only option."

"Then, we cannot allow you to leave this ridge," it replies as it begins to creep slowly forward.

I realize I have a decision to make… and must make it quickly. I can stay here and be crushed by the *Gondolas* or I can jump from the ridge and hope that I might land in the river below… and remain alive. It is slim vs. none… so I choose slim.

"Are you certain we cannot be friends?" I ask.

All fourteen *Gondolas* slowly move toward me. I turn, I run, and I jump.

It is a long way to the bottom. I see the river surging below me… and coming up fast. But even if I land in the water, I will, most likely, die. I take the only option available to me… I straighten out my body, feet down, head up, and attempt to enter the river as vertically as is possible… and just maybe, I will survive the ordeal.

I hit the river feet first. There is pain as I breach the water surface, and I am under the water... the river is deeper than expected... I continue downward... dozens of feet... maybe more... I attempt to resist the downward motion and return to the surface, but suddenly, I hit bottom, hard, and I am propelled back toward the surface. My legs are in pain... probably broken.

I soon realize I cannot make the ascent back to the surface, it is too far. I cannot move my legs and cannot hold my breath any longer. I try to hold on but I have no energy. I am already in extreme pain and now realize... that I will very shortly die. I hold on for as long as I am able, ever looking up toward the surface... but finally, I gasp for breath.

One Sim at a Time

At least the recycle process is painless… well, I designed it to be, but then, I designed most of the rest of this… experience… and that certainly has not worked out the way I had planned.

I reassemble, and it is sunny out, and I am not in the castle… Thank the *Game Master*. It is, obviously, random… just the way I programmed it back those ten odd years ago… and I am always grateful when I do not *Reset* inside the castle… since that usually ends badly.

I would like to tell you that I do not remember the pain of death… dying… being eaten alive… but, unfortunately, I *do* remember that pain and suffering. I can only hope for those occasions when the entities hit a major artery early into their meal, or take a bite of my heart, or brain… then death usually follows rather quickly… and there is not too much pain.

I will take what I can when I can. Since there is never any time to be wasted, I immediately begin my often long but mostly boring walk into the *City*. The *City* is always a surprise… since I programmed it to be that way. If memory serves, I created well over a hundred different cities… towns… metropolises… and they activate randomly, once the reset/reassembly command is executed.

As I reach the ridge, I see it… wow… this *City* is beautiful… looks like maybe the 22nd century… I'll verify later. One of the many advantages to *Sims* is there is never any pollution… unlike the real 2049, my original time reference… where everything and everywhere was polluted… too hot… almost unlivable; which is why I decided to build this game in the first place, as a way to get away from it all… to escape…

now... I must admit... the escape part works great... no complaints there!

I spot the path downward and begin my journey toward the *City*. The sun is hot... maybe 90 degrees, but then, this is the desert area, so it is supposed to be hot. As I descend the rocky recline, it starts to cool down and the glare of the sun begins to diminish. Glad I brought my continuous-adjust tinted glasses along with me. This sun is square... not my favorite shape, but then again, the shape, size, and intensity of each sun is randomly selected by the program. Wish I had that to do over again... oh well... bygones.

As I approach the *City,* I spot an outdoor market area where folks are selling goods on the street. I stop by, checking out their wares and the services being sold or bartered for. At least I am carrying my universal and unlimited *Keycard.* Hey, there has to be some advantages to being the designer of this universe... to offset the many disadvantages.

Most of the goods I observe, as I peruse through the marketplace, is std-ware, but I do spot a few '*STR*-specific' goods and begin to check them out. Maybe they have a replacement for my torch that is beginning to fail me. It being the 22nd century, I try to remember some of the features I programmed into this *STR*... but after ten years, I've pretty much forgotten. So much of what we developed is randomly generated that it is impossible to predict what an exact environment will be... until I actually begin to live and experience it.

I don't see exactly what I am looking for but do spot a few items to add to my 'bag', so purchase them and continue on toward the town. One of the (many) things I wish I had *not* created was to program anyone who accepts my universal card, or even recognizes me as the *GM*, to wink at me as they pass by or run my card through their 'Credit Balance' mechanism... whatever that happens to be, based on the *STR*. It just reminds me that this is not real... but a sophisticated *Sim*. And, since I am unable to get myself out of this *Sim*... it is very real to me, and I do not want to be continuously reminded...

I see the *City* is up ahead and decide that I will try to enjoy this adventure... experience, for as long as it lasts... or until I time-out. I arrive at the *City Gates*, provide my in-game *UnivPassPort*, or *Keycard* as it is generally known, and I'm allowed entry. That feature, use of the *Keycard* inside the *Sim*, was my brilliant marketing idea designed to support the many *in-app add-on* purchases we built into the game... and as long as I have the *Keycard*... I can get into anywhere I want, at, of course, a slight additional charge. Actually, I modeled the game's *UnivPassPort* after the real *Keycard,* which is the universally accepted means of financial exchange, in 2050. The great part is the *Keycard* works both inside and outside the *Sim* environment. So, if I ever do finally get back home, my *Keycard* will continue to work... seamless. But, the primary reason I support the 'real' keycard in my *Sim* is the simple fact that whatever the gamers... customers... charge here in my *Sim* world, comes directly out of their bank account back in the real world. We don't have to worry about credit lines or deposits... you buy it... you pay for it. It's the world's only real-to-virtual data link, and I hold three patents to prove it.

The gate dissolves in front of me, and I walk through the entrance and into the city-proper. I am both hungry and thirsty, so look around for an auto-directory, do not immediately spot one, so continue toward the downtown district. Just as I reach the outskirts of downtown, where the residential areas are usually located, a scraggly-dressed and unshaven man, maybe fifty, approaches. As he gets closer, I can smell his desperation, his despair... and his current level of poverty. I am immediately on guard and begin looking for the 'trap door'.

"Sir, can you please help. I am unable to find work or get out of this town, and I have a family to feed. We haven't eaten in days... please help."

"What is the currency in the *STR*?" I inquire.

"I have no idea what you just said. Please sir, give me five credits... at least my family will be able to eat... today."

I reach into my pocket and pull out a bill. I hand it to the unkempt man, he looks at it and then up at me. A smile forms on his weatherworn and quite scarred face, "A hundred credits... God bless you, sir." He quickly walks away, as if anticipating I might change my mind and attempt to repossess the bill.

As the beggar hustles away from me, my knees begin to feel weak, so I look for a park bench, spot one down the path... and head toward it. I take a seat... and take a deep breath. "What was that?" I ask myself.

I sit on the park bench for the better part of an hour, reflecting on what has just transpired. The dilemma, of course, is simple. I did not program any beggars into my *Sim*; why would I? This was not designed to be a touchy-feely game about feeling sorry for folks... I designed this game to be a fun adventure... or a tragic event... or a horror story... there are no beggars in my *Sim!*

Just because I am unable to exit my own *Sim* experience does not mean I have lost complete control over the environment. I programmed the vast majority of the functions and feature of the *LifeSim™* and nowhere are there beggars. It's about the adventure... moving from place to place, level to level... experiencing the good, the bad, and the horrifying aspects of life. You can get married... even have children... and you can die... so why would there not be beggars on the street? Because I didn't design them! Okay, I must calm down. Maybe one of the other programmers added them... but it was certainly not authorized.

Time to find some food and drink. I spot a sign half-way down the block, *SpaceMT*. I head there. Unfortunately, it is not a restaurant but rather an arcade. Yes, we did design arcade games within the *Sim*... why not? I look around, do not see anything that even resembles a restaurant or bar. Several folks are walking by but none are making contact. I wait...

Finally, as a good-looking female walks by, she winks, and I ask, "Is there a bar or restaurant nearby? I really need something to eat."

"Sure... I will take you there." She takes my hand and we head down the block, take a right at the corner, and I spot it down the block about half-way, and as we approach, she asks, "Do you want me to accompany you?"

"No, but thanks for guiding me." She releases my hand and is gone.

I enter the bar, look around, very few people are here. I see the restaurant side and the bar area... and I head directly to the bar and take a seat.

"What can I get you, buddy?" the bartender asks. He looks like a combo android-robot... hard to tell the difference sometimes.

"Drink of the day?" I ask.

"The *Southwest Sangria*. Small, med, or large?" he asks.

"Give me the large... half the sugar, please," I reply.

He returns and places the drink on the counter, "Card or Credits?" he states.

I hand him my *Keycard*. He touches it, winks, and heads to the register.

I am in the bar for almost an hour. Several females approach, some wink, but I ignore them. Not interested in any *SimSex* today. I am just about ready to order food when another female approaches and asks, "Is this seat taken?"

"No, help yourself." She looks at me, does not smile... and does not wink.

Her drink arrives, and I begin to watch her. She looks and acts different. It is subtle... but she is different.

"Why are you staring at me?" she asks after a few minutes, "If I am too close, I will be delighted to move to the other end of the bar."

That startles me, and I stammer, "No, you are fine, some... I was just noticing that you were..." but then I stop.

"Different... well, thank you... you are, maybe the tenth person to tell me that... today... sorry to have bothered you," she starts to get up, but I quickly recover.

"No please, stay... that is not what I meant... I just meant... that... well, never mind. Please stay. I'm sorry. My name is James Caldwell. Does that name ring a bell?" I ask.

"No, why should it? I'm Kathy Peterson. Nice to meet you... I guess."

"Most people know me as James or Jim..." I add.

"Got it."

I continue to look at Kathy... something is different about her. I can't tell what... exactly. I realize I am starting to make her uncomfortable... well, that has not happened before. I turn away and continue sipping my drink.

"I've not seen you in here before," Kathy offers, after a few silent minutes. "I thought I knew every character in this godforsaken town," she adds.

"I just arrived. Sorry if I intruded on your privacy... it won't happen again," I state as I return to my drink. We have another few minutes of awkward silence, and I am just about ready to leave the bar side and head over to the restaurant.

"May I ask you a question, Jim?" Kathy states, and she is speaking very softly... I can barely hear her.

I turn and look at her, "Certainly, Kathy, what is on your mind?"

"Well, you said you just got into town... May I ask... where did you come from?"

"I'm not sure I understand your question. I've been all over. I pop in and out without warning," I state, which is my standard, non-committal response to any unusual question.

"You do not appear to be like... the others." Kathy responds.

"Not sure what you mean, Kathy." I am sensing something emotional... but decide not to engage any more than is required to be considered 'social but not interested'. I'm getting rather hungry and need to eat soon.

"Well, for one, you have not come on to me."

"What exactly does that mean? Does everyone you meet come on to you... is that the problem?"

"Since I've arrived here, every male I meet wants to engage, and if I accept that, then... eventually... they come on to me."

"Well, I'm sorry to hear that... if I were outside, maybe I could tweak the program, but..."

"What do you mean... outside."

"Never mind. I need to leave now... nice to meet you... Kathy." I stand up, leave the bar and head over to the restaurant section. Really... that sort of uncomfortable confrontation has never happened to me before.

Evolution or Tinkering?

I take my seat in the restaurant section, and the waiter arrives to take my order. "Would you care to start with a cocktail, sir?" he asks.

"No, I'm good... just leave a menu and maybe tell me the specials of the day."

"Certainly, let me get the menu... I'll be right back." The waiter walks away and I open my *SmartComm*. I click on my *Sim App* and select *STR* to try and determine exactly where/when I landed, when I look up and there is Kathy.

"May I sit?" she asks... again no wink.

"Sure, if you want," I respond but immediately head back into my app.

"Usually, the *Sims* don't access *SmartComms*, is this a new feature?" Kathy questions.

I place my *SmartComm* on the table and look up... and into Kathy's beautiful blue eyes. "I have no idea what you are asking. I am not at liberty to share with you any of the program code... it would be unethical, and as a practical matter... might even create a dilemma."

I return to my *SmartComm*, I am able to pinpoint the date... 2217. April 5th. The *SimCity* is *IntraGalCity*, which was designed as a gateway between Earth and the local planets of Mars, Venus, and Saturn. They were part of my long-term expansion project... but, well, I got sidetracked in this damn *Sim*... and never got around to building those virtual worlds... maybe one day. I continue my research into the present *STR* but soon hear someone clearing their throat, look up... and there is Kathy.

"Oh, sorry… you are dismissed," I state and head back into my app.

"Well, that is the most arrogant and… impolite response I have ever received… what the fuck are you?"

"Not sure what you mean… you must know who I am… every *Sim* knows who I am but, unfortunately, I really don't have the time to deal with *Sims* right now. I need to plan my next movements… to try and find the *Exit Door*. If I don't plan my time here wisely… the end will arrive un-expectantly and I will be *Reset* into another *STR*… and that will probably not end well."

"What the fuck are you talking about?" Kathy asks, and I can tell she is quite irritated… and even more agitated. Maybe she needs a mood-tweak.

"For one," I respond, "I never allow my *Sim*s to curse… that is not in the standard vocab, except maybe in certain specific character-acting situations…"

"I AM NOT A SIM, YOU DUMB ASS!" Kathy replies.

Reality Inside a Sim

For the first time, I take a closer look at Kathy. I stare into her soft blue eyes, glance at her golden blonde hair... and well, yes, she looks just like one of my more popular 'Betty Series' *Sims*. "What seems to be the problem? Do you need a reset... a restart, or maybe an upgrade?" I inquire.

"What the fuck are you talking about... and who the hell are you, really? You are not a *Sim*... I have seen enough of them to understand what they can do... their limitations... so, what the hell are you!" Kathy is yelling... another un-programmed function.

"I am the creator of *LifeSim™*. But, of course, you already know that. Are you some renegade code that we need to debug... or possibly even delete?"

"Yes, please delete me from this nightmare... I thought I was just testing a *Sim*... but once I got here... I was never able to get back out."

"What do you mean testing?" I ask.

"I was hired by *FunGamesUnltd* to test the new *Sim* product they were developing."

"I am not sure I understand. I am the President and CEO on *FgU* ... and we have never met."

"No, well Brian Gantry hired me to test *Sims*... and once I went into the VR chamber... well, here I am."

"I don't even know a Brian.... how long have you been in here?" I ask.

"Not sure... maybe a year? Can you get me out? You seem to be real, well... real-*er* at least... the first human I've encountered since I arrived at this... madhouse."

"Thanks!" I reply.

"For what?" I can see Kathy is really getting agitated at this point... I may have to perform an 'in field adjustment'...

"Thanks for the compliment... 'madhouse' was absolutely the effect we were going for... but that depends on the *Sim* you select, of course... we also have the fun palace... the..."

"Please... shut the fuck up and let me think," Kathy responds, as she puts her face into her hands and begins to sob, uncontrollably... now *that* is a fully supported function, for sure.

...

As I continue to observe Kathy, I am starting to doubt my earlier assumptions regarding her... *Sim*-ness. It has been ten years since I have encountered another real human being... so I am not prepared for this... did not expect it... but must now deal with the situation.

"You could be human, I guess... or maybe an undercover agent. We created a few of them... just to mess with the game and keep it interesting," I state, not quite ready to concede the impossibility of this apparent situation.

"No, sorry, I'm not a *UC*... if you can access my employment contract, you will see I am an hourly contractor..."

"Unfortunately, I am, at the moment, trapped inside this *Sim* and cannot access anything," I reply.

"What do you mean... trapped... I don't believe you are the inventor... you seem much too stupid to have invented such a sophisticated game."

"You are correct, Kathy... I am much too stupid to invent... anything."

...

I order my food, and it arrives in the usually 10 minutes... a programmed delay to keep the realism alive. I look up and Kathy is still here... so I try to ignore her and begin to eat.

"Are you not even going to invite me to join you?" she offers once I take my first bite.

"*Sims* don't eat... they just *Sim* eating and since I don't care to deal with *Sims* at the moment... I have decided you are a program bug, and I will just ignore you... and soon you will go away."

Well that does not go as expected. Kathy stands, walks over, and slaps me hard across the face. "Can a *Sim* do that?" she asks as she returns to her seat.

Well, I must admit... while it is possible to feel pain from a *Sim*... and I've had hundreds of *Entities* attacking me to prove that... never has one of the female *Sims* struck me. They are not programmed to do that... except in certain rare instances... maybe I need to rethink the situation.

...

I check my watch and calculate how long Kathy and I have been together. Good, it's been almost an hour, so I wait for the hourly refresh cycle to commence... but, still, Kathy remains seated at the table. Hum... okay, maybe it's time to talk. "Do you have a home or place we can go to talk?" I ask.

"Not until you offer me some food... I am starving."

"Sorry... waiter... whatever Kathy wants... get it and charge it to my account."

Kathy eats like no *Sim* I've ever encountered before. She orders wine... and I join in on that.

Finally, Kathy seems satisfied. "Thank you, Jim. That was the best meal I've had in a while... since I ran out of *Test Credits* almost four months back, I've been living off... well *stealing* would be the proper term... I have been stealing food whenever I can."

Still not quite convinced, I simply nod... and continue to scan her model, attempting to locate the trigger that just may allow me to deactivate her. Obviously, she is a run-away... it happens every now and then... and they have been known to cause some major damage.

"I acquired this visitor's cube over in the residential section, which allows me to continue to exist in this *Sim* environment. Let's go there... and we can talk further."

I pay the check (failure to pay for goods or services opens a whole new event-driven scenario that I choose not to get into at this point), follow Kathy out of the restaurant, we walk down the street, and finally come to a hotel. "I checked in here once I arrived in this... hell hole... and so far, they have not asked me for any real money."

"No, if you are a 'guest', then they would not. You most likely paid up front, and the only extra charges are the add-ons you agreed to," I offer. "You probably did not check the 'unlimited meals/entertainment' box on the app... and therefore at a certain point, based upon either time spent onsite or total credits expended... you would be cut off from..."

"Well, thanks for that small consolation prize... but, how the hell do I get out of here?"

...

"Well, Kathy, assuming you *are* real... and, I am not yet convinced of that improbable scenario, then I would have to say... you are royally fucked!"

"There must be an off switch or *Exit Door* somewhere," Kathy replies as she opens a bottle of wine and pours two drinks.

"Ice with mine, please," I request.

"I don't have any ice... make do!" she responds.

"Touchy, are we?"

"Don't make me hit you again... and if you really are the inventor of this... this horror story... I may do a lot worse than just hit you!"

"Like what... I'm been killed, eaten, beaten, tortured, mutilated, set afire, buried underground... had fingers, toes, arms, and legs severed... I'm really not too concerned with any harm you may cause."

Kathy slams the drink on the table, "You are such a bastard... maybe you really did create this nightmare... so if you did, how can I get out? ...please... no more games..."

"First, I'm still not convinced that you are real. No offense, but you remind me a lot of the Betty Model... I designed that one myself. She did not get the arrogance chip... but maybe that was added later on. After all, I've been in here for ten years... a lot could have happened. Just today, for example... I met a beggar on the street... can you believe that?" I respond as I take my first sip of wine.

"Probably some other tester who got stuck inside this torture chamber," Kathy replies. I am kind of liking her quick wit... but that too was not programmed into the Betty Model... they were designed to be sweet, loving... accommodating.

"No, actually, the torture chamber is another *Sim* altogether... I had that one in Beta before I..."

"Enough! I've had enough... get the hell out of my hotel... whoever or whatever the fuck you are!" Kathy is now standing over me, shouting, her face is red... she is angry, agitated... almost out of control.

The truth finally arrives... and hits me square in the center of my tiny and currently underused brain... "You are real... aren't you? My Betty Model would never react that way.... Where did you say you came from...? I really wasn't listening back then... I was too concerned with my own survival to deal with..."

Kathy places her hand over my mouth, and I cease talking. "If you will shut up... for just a moment... I will tell you how I got here... can you do that? Please?"

She removes her hand, slowly, and I nod... but say nothing. "As I said earlier, I was hired as a *Sim Tester*. I wasn't given a lot of data, but I knew there had been some trouble with the *Sim*... that scuttlebutt had been going around the gaming world for several years. I was told that for $250 credits an hour, I did not get to ask questions, only to test the software... from inside the *Sim.*"

I take a final sip and finish my drink. Without asking, I return to the kitchen, pour myself another glass of wine, this one all the way to the top, and return.

"Where's mine... obviously, you've lost all manners in the last... ten years, I believe you said, assuming you ever had any... which, at this point, I believe that assertion is quite doubtful." I head back to the kitchen, fill up Kathy's glass, return, gently place the glass on the table and return to my seat.

"Better… and thanks… now where was I? Oh yea, they deposited a 5k credit chip into my account…. And all I had to do to earn that sizable fee was to enter the S*im*, walk around for a couple of days, take notes on what I found… and then report the results back to them."

"So how were you supposed to return… from the *Sim*…" I ask, feeling a bit anxious but also hopeful.

"They said they would control that end. I asked a few follow-up questions but was never given any exact details, only vague responses. At the time, I was not too concerned… how could you not come back from a *Sim*… I mean… really?"

"My thoughts exactly," I reply.

Gaining a Common Understanding

"So were you given any device to… uh… record your notes on?"

"Yes, they had a special tablet with several apps that I was supposed to access and record my notes, reactions, opinions."

Key question… "And where is this tablet… right now, Kathy? …that could be our ticket home," I state, trying to keep any emotion out of my voice.

"Well, I'm getting there… so bear with me… I did walk through various sceneries… for almost a week… at least it seemed like a week. I took daily surveys, filed reports, and the app indicated they were 'posted', so I felt that I was still, somewhat, in communications with the outside world."

"Did they give you any other device to communicate with them?"

"No, they told me that one of the primary purposes of the *LifeSim*™ was to get away… and lose connection with the 'real world'."

"Yea, which was one of my big ideas…" I respond as I begin to reflect on what Kathy has been telling me.

"Are you still here, Jim?" Kathy asks.

I look up, "Sorry, I believe I zoned out for a moment… continue with your story."

"Does that happen often… the zoning out part?" she asks.

"Yes, unfortunately, much too often."

…

"Okay, so after a week I was supposed to get a signal, via the tablet, telling me it was time to depart. I was to walk back to my point of entry... and then wait."

"And what happened?" I ask.

"I received the signal... and a thirty minute countdown. I hurried over to my point of entry... the gates to the *SimCity*, and waited."

"Then what happened?"

"At exactly 00:00:00, as I looked at the tablet... it disappeared... but, unfortunately, I remained. That was ten months ago... according to my time calculations, which I will admit... are not exact."

I go back into thought... is there any new information here I can use? ...to possibly get us out of here... and back to reality? "What did you do next?" I ask.

"Oh, I stayed right there at the gate, barely moving... for at least an hour. After about ten minutes, I began to panic and wanted to run... but where would I run to... so I stayed and I waited..."

We've been at this now for over an hour. We are both tired. "Okay, I am not sure how much longer I will be in the *STR*, but...."

"What's an *STR*?" Kathy asks.

"Space Time Reference. Each 'new adventure' is encased or encompassed... depending how you want to look at it, in its own *STR*. Some adventures are in the past, some in the future... that sort of thing. That was the brilliant, and patent pending, part of my design... never been done before."

"And why is that important?"

"It's just a reference point... the *Sims* were created to cover a period of a couple of thousand years... so the *STR* just indicates which timeline you ended up going to... on that specific adventure."

"So, are you saying... we are traveling through time...? I just assumed this was just a video game... a simulated environment... no one told me..."

"Now, don't panic... take a deep breath, and I'll attempt to explain."

"No... not right now. I need to get out of here... get some fresh air... or maybe that is *Sim* air..."

"Okay, but do you want to meet again... and continue this conversation?" I ask.

"Oh, you are not leaving my side or my sight. No way... you are the first real thing that has happened to me since I got here."

"Well, I cannot guarantee how long I will remain in the *STR*. It varies by *Sim*. Time is another random factor in the adventure."

"So, do you have any idea... of the *Time* variable?" Kathy asks.

"Anywhere from several days to several weeks. The shortest, not counting those times I actually die, is about twelve hours... the longest would be maybe thirty days."

"So, we should have some time to figure this out... before you... disappear?" Kathy asks.

"Yes," I respond.

"I want to ask what it feels like to die in a *Sim*... but I really don't want to know."

"Good... and I don't want to tell you. Now, just to verify... you've been in this specific *Sim* for almost a year... and you've never been reset or restarted... is that correct?"

"Yes, I've been in this city for close to a year. I live here... I survive, mostly. I never leave."

"Have you ever attempted to leave the city?" I inquire.

"Yes, I can get to the main gate but not further."

"What happens once you get to the gate?"

"The gate watchman asks for my *Keycard* and I don't have a card... so he does not allow the gate to open. What stupid fuck would design a game where you could not leave a section of it...?"

"Uh... I would be the stupid fuck who designed that... feature... it was an attempt to get 'in-game add-ons'... extra money from the game participants."

"So, not only are you a dumb fuck–ass hole... but a greedy bastard to boot?" Kathy asks.

"Guilty on both counts," I reply.

Getting to Know You

Kathy decides to walk the streets… as she often does when she is sad, depressed, agitated… or simply cannot sleep. "I need the physical exercise. At first, I figured I could sit around all day… do nothing… but soon learned that even in this damn *Sim*, I need to exercise my body… and my mind."

"So what do you do to exercise your mind?" I inquire as we continue our walk around the *City*.

"I read… there is a very nice virtual library over there a few blocks, and I play video games… lots of video games. Actually, I hold a few gaming records."

"Really… how surprising… I mean… congratulations! What else do you do in your spare time?"

"You are fairly weak in the arts area… no museums or art galleries."

"Yea, well, honestly, most gamers aren't the least bit interested in art galleries… or museums… or anything that even smacks of culture. Do you go out at night… or just during the day?" I ask… yes it's a leading question.

"Oh, I tried going out a couple of times at night…pretty much scared the shit out of me. The first zombie I encountered chased me all the way back to my hotel room. I tried one other time… but kept getting glimpses of these dark winged creatures… so returned home and stayed there."

"Good, if one of those winged creatures had caught you, you would understand the pain associated with virtual death," I respond. "It seemed like a good idea at the time I created them but now… not so much."

"I'll leave that one alone… for now. I am feeling better, and there is the *Big6* game room up ahead… would you care to step inside and let me show you how good I've gotten at this gaming-thing?" Kathy asks.

"I'm game… lead the way."

...

Now, in my own defense… I did not create most of the games in the arcade… but did contribute a few ideas along the way. Needless to say, Kathy beat the shit out of me every game we played. Now again, she got to pick the game… but I must say, I was rather impressed with her performance. "Where to next?" I ask, once she's whipped my ass for maybe the tenth time.

"I'm thirsty… and since you have the unlimited *Keycard* card… I'll let you buy me a drink at the bar down the street. I used to go there in the early days, but one time, I was told I had exceeded my credit limit… and they were not very nice when I told them I didn't have any money to pay the check."

"Yes, unfortunately, I wrote the 'non-payment scenario'. Which one did you get… the big bouncer, the ten-minute cop ride to jail, or the trap door into the dudgeon?" I ask.

"Oh, I was able to talk my way out of it… apparently there are ways to defeat the system…"

"Hum, no, there is no way to defeat the system… if you don't pay, then a random 'punishment' is generated… and something bad happens to you…"

"Not if you offer to give the bartender a special tip…"

"The bartenders are all android-robots… they cannot perform sex of any kind. I would have thought you knew that… everyone knows that," I respond, rather put off by the very insinuation.

"Ah, yes, and that caused the dilemma," Kathy responds as a small smile begins to creep across her cute and sparsely freckled face.

"What do you mean?" I ask.

"Had the bartender been a human *Sim*, I would not have offered, understanding that guests and *Sims* are capable of performing virtual sex inside the *VR*. However, based on the size, shape, and non-gender specific make-up of the bartender, I assumed he, she, or it could not perform *SimSex*... so I decided to ask for sex... as compensation for the bar tab... and see how it reacted."

I'm afraid to ask, "And what was the reaction?"

"As I had hoped, it shut down... apparently, it had not been programmed for that specific request, had no answer, so shut itself down."

"So what did you do then?" I ask.

"Ran like hell... what you think? That was the first time I stole anything... I saw a bottle of good scotch on the counter... so I picked it up and got the hell out of there."

"Clever girl..." I respond, as I begin to think about the ramifications of that declaration.

"Okay, let's go to that bar... and see if anyone recognizes you," I add as I take Kathy's hand and we head into the *Caveman Cavern* Bar. "I'm not worried," Kathy replies, "I now know the owner..."

...

We take a seat at the bar and an android-robot approaches, "Welcome... and what will it be... lady... gentleman...?" it asks.

"Wine for me," I reply.

"Scotch," Kathy replies, "You guys have good scotch." The bartender nods, turns, heads over and begins pouring the drinks.

"Getting a little arrogant, are we?" I inquire.

"Hey, I need to get something good out of all of the shit I've had to endure this last year."

The bartender returns, drinks in hand, and places them on the counter before us, "Would you care to order food... or just relax and enjoy?" it asks.

Kathy begins to taunt, "Oh, you don't remember me, such a pity... but my offer still stands..."

"I do not understand the question?" it responds and begins to move away... as programmed.

"Don't fuck with the hired help," I offer. "You won... you don't need to rub it in."

"Oh, but I do… I get so little satisfaction out of this… *Sim*… I will take my delight… and my revenge, whenever and wherever I can get it."

…

We have several drinks in the *CC* bar, and then I decide it is time to leave. "It will be dark soon… so we had better get back to the hotel… before the zombies come out," I state as I look down at my watch.

"You know what that reminds me of," Kathy states as she stands, stretches, and gets prepared to depart.

I pay the check, the bartender nods, "Have a great evening… but be careful out there."

"No, what does that remind you of?" I ask as we exit the bar, hand in hand.

"That ancient Charlton Heston movie… you know that classic… from way back in the 1970s… what was the name of that film?" she asks.

"Soylent Green?" I respond, not willing to disclose that I know exactly what film she is referring to.

"No… that's not it… that one was about the end of the world caused by global warming I believe… this one was the end of the world… there were zombies… vampires… I believe a nuclear war caused that apocalyptic event."

I wait while she thinks, but finally decide to come clean. "It was 'The Omega Man'… 1971."

"How did you know that?" Kathy asks.

"I had rather not say," I reply.

It is beginning to get dark, and I increase my pace, "Let's get home… they will be out shortly… and we do not want to be here once they arrive." I take Kathy's hand, and we head back to the hotel.

Reaching an Accommodation

We make it back to the hotel before the sun is completely below the horizon.

"Well, that was actually fun, James… thanks. At least having someone with me… someone real and unpredictable to talk to… is a definite improvement. I have some food… a little I stole last week. But unfortunately, I am out of wine… we drank the last of it this afternoon."

"I'm fine… so what's next… do you want more information… or just to relax and enjoy?" I ask.

"That sounds rather leading… but let's go with door number two… relax and enjoy," she responds.

I consume a couple of glasses of water, and Kathy has something that looks and feels like cheese… but tastes more like cardboard, "Where did you steal this?" I inquire.

"Can't remember, but it has no taste. But, anything we consume, apparently, sustains us… not sure why that is."

"Necessity," I reply. "We were able to come up with a synthetic formula that reacts the same in both the real and virtual world. Some of it tastes like food… and some… taste like cardboard… or worse."

I continue, "What do you usually do at night? We did not program TV in this *Sim*… mostly, I created this *Sim* so the guys could spend their evenings hunting zombies or running from them… attempting to avoid death. We have lots of hot autos out there… and the guys can drive them… just like in the movie. Some cars have weapons, and we need to remember that in case we are out too late and get into trouble. All they have to do is insert their *Keycard*… agree to the slight up-charge… and they are on their way."

"Oh, so you stole that idea from 'The Omega Man' movie?" Kathy asks.

"Well, I would not use the term 'stole'... that movie was back in the 70s... but we did borrow a few concepts... the zombies, the night attacks, some of the chases... but don't worry... no zombies will actually come knocking on your door... trying to get in... unless you purchased that upgrade and checked the appropriate boxes."

...

"Let's talk more tomorrow, James," Kathy states, about midnight, "You can sleep over there on the couch... if you wake early, there is coffee... or at least it tastes a little like coffee... in the pantry in the kitchen... good night."

...

It takes a while for sleep to come. I have mostly pleasant thoughts and for some reason... a renewed hope.

I awake and do smell the coffee... and head toward the kitchen. Kathy has her coffee in hand... and points toward the dispenser. I quickly locate a mug, press the appropriate buttons, and the coffee begins pouring into my cup. I take the seat next to Kathy and take my first sip. It is the usual... and not bad... maybe I've gotten accustom to *Sim*-coffee after ten years.

Kathy is reading one of the books from the virtual library and so I sit, drink my coffee, and think. Finally, after maybe thirty minutes, I decide to open the dialog, "I have no idea how long I will remain in this timeline, so what do you need to know... to help you..."

"I thought I made that quite clear yesterday... I need to find a way out of this godforsaken shit-hole... and if you really are the creator... inventor... then it is your responsibility and moral obligation to assist me in getting the fuck out of here."

Well, there is no uncertainty or ambiguities in that declaration... I have been put on notice, for sure. "Okay, I will try, but I must remind you. I've been trapped here for ten years... have not found a way out... so how, exactly, am I supposed to help you find your way home?"

"Your problem… not mine," Kathy responds without looking up from her book.

"Actually, Kathy, while I greatly sympathize with your dire situation, I am not the one who put you into this *Sim*… and it is not my responsibility to get you out of it."

"So, day two of you being the *Bastard*?" she responds.

"So, day two of you being the *Bitch*?" I reply.

Exploring the City

We continue without speaking. While I have no immediate plans to dump the bitch currently seated at the table to the left of me, I have absolutely zero desire to continue to engage with her. I understand her frustration... but seriously, I have my own survival issues. And, whether I like it or not, one of these days, in the not too distant future, I will be reset... and will open my eyes in another of the many virtual reality worlds that I, and others, created.

"Okay, then," I begin, "I need to go out, scout around and look for some environment clues... reference points, if you will."

"Do you always talk like that?" Kathy asks, as she finally looks up from her book and sets it gently on the table.

"Talk like what? Is this yet another jab... accusation, to try and let me know that you are royally pissed at being trapped here? I get it, Kathy... I've gotten it for ten years now. Okay, so I invented this VR game.... But I did not imprison you inside of it... why would I? As far as I am concerned... you can leave at any time... and quite frankly... the sooner the better. Sorry... but I must go now.... Hope to see you around... NOT!"

I decide that now is an excellent time to leave, and so I do. Once I'm out on the street, I begin to scan the area, looking for clues. I access my *SmartComm* and re-scan the area. The *Sim* is identified as *ADV-ZQuest12*. I link to the details page and begin reading. Yes, this is the world I created based on a combo of 'The Omega Man'... and some ideas JoAnne and I came up with.

Damn, I have not thought of JoAnne in almost a year. God, I do miss her. I'm certain that by now, she's moved on...

forgotten all about me… and who can blame her. I wonder if she even attempted to try and determine what happened to me. My one week final *Beta-Sim* test… has now lasted well over ten years. I need to forget JoAnne… because even if I do finally get back home, there is little or no possibility she will be there with open arms, and open legs, to greet me.

Daytime in most of the monster-based *Sims* is fairly safe. We do have a few 'trap doors' as we call them but these are few and far between. For the most part, this *Sim* is about the night time… during the daylight hours, you are on your own to explore the city, shop around, pick up a virtual hooker (if you are so inclined), visit one of the many bars or spas in the area, play at any of the several arcades… or simply remain in your hotel room and recuperate from your wild night of 'Zombie Hunting'.

Now, as I think back, I must tell you about this clever in-app *add-on* I created. It's never been tried before… I'll make it short. If you do get eaten or clawed to death by a zombie (or any of the other randomly-generated monsters), then you have to pay an additional fee to return to the game. Now, how clever is that? Even if you paid for a full three day-three night package… if you are killed,… then it costs up to a hundred credits to return to the game, or be 'reinstated'. Of course, that was all legal… and is noted in the twenty-two page contract you sign… somewhere down there on page 18 or 19… I can't remember exactly. I expect that add-on alone to net me a hundred-million a year… assuming I ever get out of here and get this game on the market.

It is now 2PM; I've explored a good portion of the city… but have obtained no new clues that might help me find the *Exit Door*. I spot a bar up the way, so head over. I should have known, with a name like *A Bar*, it would either be filled with androids or ass-holes… but at least it's androids and aliens. Oh yea, they come in a variety of sizes and shapes. And yes, we did steal that idea from the original *Star Wars*™ movie. In my opinion, at least, these ideas come from our guides somewhere out there in the universe and it is up to each individual to pick up the information and use it as we see fit. Since I was not even alive when the Star War movies were created… then how could

I have picked up the information? Okay, so, I borrow a piece here, a concept there... and soon... I have a VR world that anyone could be proud of... or rather terrified of. That's my story and I'm sticking with it.

I have to actually push and shove my way up to the bar. A few of the uglier aliens get in my face along the way, but I simply push them aside and continue toward the bar. Finally I arrive, and an eight-legged, three-eyed monster states, "Ⴎⅇ⑂⋇⌧✕⌧⏛ ◆⋇⩷⋇⌧Ⅲ⏛⎕✦"

My in-app translator add-in instantly interprets, "What is your pleasure?"

"Scotch!" I shout, mainly because it is super noisy in here. Everyone (or maybe it's everything) is talking at once... and I do not understand a word. Now, just to keep your expectations at a manageable level, do not expect Hans Solo to show up... no, we did not pay that fee... and our designers made each and every alien from scratch... except for those few that came out of the PD 50's horror/Sci-Fi movies. My scotch arrives... and it tastes like scotch... which is the reason I often order it. Do not try the Mexican Beers... they are awful.

It is much too noisy, so after consuming my scotch (at least the alcohol effects are real... We do add actual grain alcohol to the *Sim*-drinks), I decide to leave. I pay my tab and if the bartender actually had any eyes... I'm certain he would have winked. Leaving the bar is almost as difficult as getting in here. A pair of twin aliens... four foot tall, green... and quite ugly, block my way toward the door. I stop. The other aliens look our way and slowly move away from us. Very soon, it is just me and the two... rather short, but wiry aliens.

Now if I were not in a hurry... and had not been through a similar scenario, maybe a dozen times before, I might have tried to reason with them... but I'm really not in the mood, so I simply quick-kick each alien in the head, they fall, hit the wall or floor, and I walk out the door.

I stop into a *Burger Barn*, have a quick bite, and head back into town. By 4:30PM, I am getting tired and decide to look for a place to stay the night (as far away from Kathy as I can get... obviously). I check one of the street directories, and there is a hotel up ahead, maybe three blocks. I head in that direction but soon, begin to regret that decision. As I head out of the main portion of the city… I head into a sleazy little burrow of town. The buildings begin to look creepy, most need a paint job or at least some whitewash… but I continue moving in the direction of the hotel. I see it up ahead… and stop in my tracks. It looks to be the exact hotel from the movie *Psycho*… yea the Bates Motel… that's it. Damn, I had no idea we stole that one… or maybe we licensed it… let's go with that for now.

No, I decide I'm not staying at the Bates Motel tonight… or any night for that matter. I turn to head back into town. Oops… zombies… but it isn't even dark yet… I have several more hours before sunset. Nonetheless, there are zombies, blocking my path forward… oh this must be a 'trap door'. Okay, well, I must deal with it regardless. There is no use even trying to communicate with zombies, all they want is your blood… your brain… heart or any other vital organ that you might be fond of.

I am hopeful that the rule of hotel-safety remains in force and decide that the Bates Hotel could not possibly be worse that a gang of blood-sucking zombies so I turn and quickly make my way toward the hotel. Now the good thing about zombies, as we all know… is that they are slow as shit. How they ever catch a meal… I have no idea… and do not care to find out.

I enter the hotel… thank God, Anthony Perkins is *not* standing behind the front desk. Rather, a lovely young lady… in her early twenties… blond… green eyes… and not-too-shabby looking (for the Bates Motel). "May I assist you?" she states, in an eerie but also kind of sexy voice.

"Yes, I need a room… just for the night… high floor… no view."

"Yes, sir… that will be a hundred credits."

I pull out my *UnivCard*, hand it to her, she takes it… does not wink and announces, "The hundred credits is in addition to your normal per-night fee… just so you understand."

Another in-app add-on… when will this end? "But I purchased the full deluxe package," I state.

"Sorry, but I guess you have a choice… pay the fee or return to the streets… and take your chances with the zombies."

"Run it," I state.

...

I am in my room. My view is of the back alley. Of course, there is no bar or restaurant in the Bates Motel… why would there be? I decide just to stay in my room… wait it out and head out and back into the *City*, at first light in the morning.

No such luck. It is not long before the sun goes down and the full moon arrives. I begin to hear the screams, shouts… people begging… then I hear bone and flesh being crunched… eaten… devoured. Oh, trust me, I know exactly what that sounds like. I look out my window… and the place is crawling with zombies… and other unimaginable monsters, many I have never seen before. While I know this is only a *Sim*… that does not prevent me from being scared shitless. But of course, that is the point. Everyone who enters understands it's a *Sim*… but our intent is to scare the holy-shit out of you… and mine leaves rather quickly that evening.

I know I'm safe in my room, so try to relax. After a few hours, the screams, moans, and groans begin to diminish and I am finally able to nod off. I awake to a loud banging sound… I jump up… and hear it again… it is the door. I decide to stand very still… not move and just listen. The banging re-commences… and this time it is much louder… and I can hear the moans and the groans of the monsters waiting on the other side of the door.

I decide to do nothing… no way they will break the door down and get at me… we are safe in our rooms… that is part of the standard agreement and is not a user-overrideable option.

It takes another few minutes but finally, the banging stops and all is quiet outside the door. I wait another ten minutes, just to be certain. Hearing nothing, I decide to take a look. Of course, the chain is securely on the door, so I unlock it, slowly open the door and peek out into the hallway.

At least a dozen zombies attempt to kick the door in and quickly succeeding, they rush me… One grabs me and I receive a large bite on my left arm. I push it off me but the others are right behind. I have little choice, so I run toward the back of the room and literally jump through the rear window. I hear the breaking of the glass as I jump through and immediately, hit the porch roof below… probably saving me. I bounce and then hit the street below. Damn that hurts. I am certain my arm is broken.

I awake and the sun is shining... I shade my eyes from the glare and try to get to my feet. No way that is going to happen. My left arm contains several large bite marks and is bleeding, and my right ankle is twisted… maybe broken as well. I attempt to stand, and on the third try… I succeed, somewhat. I am in an alley, so I place my right hand against the wall… and slowly begin to move out of the alley and back toward the *City*.

It takes an hour to navigate the several blocks and arrive back in the city-proper… but where to now? I cannot go back to Kathy… that is far worse than a few zombie bites. I look over at my left arm, which is now aching… and once again it is bleeding and it seems to already be swelling… maybe infected. My last thought, before I pass out is… 'You can't get an infection from a virtual zombie bite…'

Forming an Alliance

I awake and see an angel looking down at me. Maybe, finally, I have died and gone to heaven... not so sure that is a bad thing. But as the angel comes into focus, I see that it is Kathy. Now, I'm thinking, maybe I did, finally, die... and this is really hell....

...

I feel something warm on my face... I try to move my left hand... but cannot, so I move my right hand up to my face... it is a wet cloth... warm... feels good. I decide that regardless of whether I am in hell or heaven... I am not, at the moment, in pain.

...

As my eyes begin to focus, I see Kathy in the kitchen... doing something... not sure what... but decide that now would be a good time to relocate... so I attempt to get out of bed... but only succeed in falling face first onto the floor.

"What the fuck are you doing, James? ...can you not even remain in bed?"

I slowly roll onto my side. I look up and there is Kathy. I am barely able to mumble, "God, please forgive me for all my many sins... I had no idea I was so bad that you had to send me to virtual hell. Please... give me another chance... I promise to do better."

"Stop your muttering and help me get you back to bed. Shit, your arm is bleeding again. Damn it, James, I don't have any blood so a transfusion is out of the question. Here, let me change that bandage… sorry but I have to use your tee shirt… *you* don't supply bandages in the *VR Sim*."

…

I am semi-awake and I attempt to follow the dialog and the procedure, as it unfolds. But I have difficulty. I must have a fever… and then remember, "We do support fever remedies… they are available at the Rx stores… every few blocks…"

"Don't you think that after a year… I know where the aspirins are? Yes, you do have a fever… but it is beginning to come back down… it was almost 106… I was very worried."

"Sorry to have put you through this… additional trouble… feel free to leave at any time… once I die… I reset and then I'll be rid of you forever…"

As I make that statement, I deeply regret it, "I didn't mean that…"

"Yes, you did, but I probably deserved it. Yes, I blame you for everything bad that has happened to me this last year… and for that, I apologize."

What, an apology? Maybe, I died and went to heaven after all.

…

"Here, drink this… you are dehydrated as well as infected. I acquired some over-the-counter antibiotics… but they don't seem to be working. Your arm is very red… swollen. Is that even possible?"

"No, it is not possible to get an infection from a virtual zombie bite," I reply.

"Oh, well, then… it must be a *virtual* infection… excuse me for caring." Kathy replies, but the bite in her voice seems to be gone.

"Sorry… I did not mean to bite the hand that feeds me… pun intended," I reply.

"You really are weird... not sure I've ever met anyone exactly like you before," Kathy offers.

"And why would you want to?" I respond.

"Excellent point. So, let me ask this... the vampires can kill you but not give you an infection, not sure I understand that."

"First off, they are not vampires, they are zombies... there is a subtle but distinct difference between..."

"Never mind the techno-babble... just answer my question... please?"

"Okay, yes your assumption is correct. The monsters, and even some of the seemingly harmless looking animals can kill you inside the *Sim*... and it feels like a very painful death. Inside the *Sim*, we are able to access the pain centers inside the brain and stimulate those to make you think you are in pain. The death is simply a reset/restart. Your game *VR*-self is reset, and placed back into the game, usually, at a random location decided by the game itself, but, of course, you control a great deal of the randomness based upon how you answered the questionnaire... attached to the app you signed when you agreed to the terms and conditions. The primary condition, of course, is 'thou shall never sue the game owners if anything goes wrong.'" I have more to say but need, at some point, to stop and take a breath.

"A simple yes or no would have sufficed," Kathy replies.

"I never answer any questions with a simple yes or no... actually there are very few simple answers. If you break the request down into its individual components... and answer each component separately, you can begin to..."

"Moving on... so, that leads me to my follow-up question... how can you get an infection from a virtual zombie bite?"

"You can't," I respond, succinctly.

...

I am, finally, able to sit up. My left arm looks and feels terrible. It remains red and swollen. "I am very concerned, James. Your arm is not getting any better... I've checked with the two Rx stores in the area but they have nothing else... just aspirin and synthetic antibiotics… and they don't seem to be working."

"Okay, I guess it's time to cut the arm off. I have a virtual saw over there… somewhere."

"Wow… even when you are possibly dying, you remain an ass-hole."

"Let me remind you… in the past ten years… I've died hundreds of times… maybe even thousands. I am used to it by now. But don't kid yourself. Every time I die… there is pain… sometimes it's quick… but sometimes it takes days. I've endured a lot worse than this…"

"Okay, sorry I asked. I realize I did not treat you as an ally when we first met, and James, for that, I am sorry. But… that was yesterday… can we start over… try again? I believe that we need each other."

"Not sure I can endear the continued grief that follows you around," I reply.

"Okay, I deserved that too… but we need to stop this… bantering. I promise… no more jabs, insults, put downs… can you also agree?"

I have to think about that for a moment. "Okay… I can try going down that road… and see where it leads us."

"Do you ever answer a question with just yes… or no?"

"No."

Ever-Changing Reality

I decide to rethink my absolute and unequivocal hatred for Kathy. Allies vs. adversaries… that should be a no-brainer. "I am not sure what we can accomplish… I am subject to a reset/restart anytime now. Maybe, the best we can do is kiss and make up," I offer.

"I am not attracted to you sexually, James," Kathy replies.

"My God, Kathy, I was not coming on to you… sorry I used the 'kiss and make up' cliché. Besides, you are simply *not* my type."

"And what is your type?" she responds.

"I prefer real humans… caring and compassionate humans… and not ass-holes who think they know everything, when, in actuality… they know dip-shit. Again, sorry… but you asked."

All is quiet for a while and for that, I am grateful. I begin to think about my transition into the next reality… will I really be sorry to see Kathy go? Damn, the answer comes back loud and clear… NO!

…

It takes several more days but finally, the swelling in my arm begins to diminish, my temp returns to normal, and I believe I will survive. I still do not understand the 'why' behind the infection… it is simply not possible to get any sort of permanent scar, infection, or internal disorder from being bitten, eaten, or otherwise consumed by one of the monsters in my *Sim*. I mean, basically, once we are inside the *Sim*… we too… are virtual. We have been pixelized, and the only way to return to real-life is to exit the *Sim* through one of the many escape doorways or pre-programmed exit portals. That is the part I'm having the most difficulty with, and, apparently, so is Kathy. I've been looking for the escape doorway for ten years now… and simply can't find it.

So, back to the original question… the short answer is… you can't get an infection inside the *Sim*, unless that is one of the 'special effects' you signed up for… we do have those in-app add-ons… BTW.

···

Kathy does not spend a great deal of time with me during these next few days… I understand that. But finally, on, I believe day five of us being together, she speaks, "I think you are finally on the mend, so I would appreciate it if you would leave now and go find your own hotel room. I realize you will be exiting this *Sim* soon… and I'm not sure I can handle that… after all."

"After all of what?" I respond.

"After all of the shit you've put me through… I will still miss you."

I have to think about that for a few moments. I come up with several retorts… some of which are so clever… but for some reason, I am no longer feeling vindictive… hostile. "I'm sorry… honestly… I will miss you. It has been… *different*…"

"Hell is different than heaven … is that what you mean?"

"No, that is not what I mean."

"Then what do you mean?"

"What do you care? Does it really matter?"

"Yes, James, it matters!"

"Okay… I'll begin looking for a new place to live… but will not be returning to the Bates Motel… that is a certainty. BTW, how did you find me anyway…? I assumed you had given me the 'good riddance' farewell and was glad I was out of your life. But… I wake up… and there you are."

"Oh, I didn't find you, you found me. You were lying at the entrance to my hotel; I almost tripped over you on my way to… lunch."

…

After four or five days… being cramped up in these tiny quarters, it is time for both of us to leave the hotel room… we have several hours before sunset. I am getting some of my strength back and we both need to eat.

"Personally, I could use several, strong drinks. Let's go next door to the pub… have some drinks… eat… and just try to relax," I suggest.

"Sounds good. While we are out… you can begin looking for a new place to stay…"

We leave the hotel and walk the half block to *El Bistro*. We arrive, and for a change… everyone in the bar appears to be humans. *Sims*, yes, but at least they are human *Sims*.

"Wine, please," Kathy orders.

"Same for me," I reply.

"Thought you were a scotch drinker," Kathy points out.

"I am not a one trick pony, I have lots of levels…"

"Good to know… but I'll let that pass, for now."

Our drinks arrive and we begin to sip them. It takes a while but we both manage to relax. I am actually beginning to enjoy myself. The bartender is a real, human *Sim*… which is kind of unusual… but not strictly forbidden.

After a few glasses of wine, the bartender approaches, "Would you like some food? You've been drinking for a while and I am becoming concerned regarding your alcohol levels."

I cannot allow that remark to pass unanswered, "Since we will not be driving anywhere this afternoon, then I don't think our alcohol level is any of your concern… another round… if you will!"

The bartender leaves, Kathy looks at me, and actually smiles… I did not know she could even do that. "Good retort, James. I am so sick and tired of bartenders telling me I've had enough… did you program that? Just asking… not judging."

"No, I am not sure where that came from. There are a certain number of drinks per day, allocated to each guest, depending on the package they selected, and after that point, the bartender begins to inquire. But that is strictly a 'financial' thing and not a sobriety concern. Actually, it is a known fact that folks who have had too much to drink usually spend more credits than those who remain sober. So, actually... we encourage our guests to drink... and if they do end up causing any damage, then well, there is always that *Keycard*."

"Sorry I asked," Kathy replies.

I realize I am becoming... sorry... have become, an extremely boring person. But, in my defense... I've been in this *Sim* for almost ten years... if I ever had any communication skills... which is doubtful... they have long since vanished... evaporated. I am, basically, a thinker, planner... a doer. I have never been a people person. I take a deep breath and restart.

"We did not program any specific attitude into the waiters or bartenders, but we did provide them with the ability to *learn*. Maybe that is what's happening... they are learning and reacting."

"Okay, I understand that... but what are they reacting to? According to what I understand and what you've told me... this game has never actually gone online. When I was contracted, I was told it was still in *Beta*... and you confirmed that. So what could they learn... and from whom?"

Well, that is a good question, and will need to consider before responding. "Let me contemplate... and consider before answering," I respond.

We continue hanging out and talking, but do, eventually, order some lunch. The bartender seems relieved. I would like to place him in virtual maintenance mode, run some diagnostics... but decide just to let it go... it is such a minor thing. But then, suddenly, I remember the beggar on the street that first morning, "Have you encountered anyone else... since you've been here, whom you thought might be real and not a *Sim*? Not part of the game... the adventure...?" I ask once our food arrives, and Kathy has a mouthful of *Sim*-chicken to chew on.

She chews for a moment, thinking but then replies, "No, I don't believe so. I was told to expect everything to appear real... and by God it does that... some of it is much too real."

"Thanks," I reply.

"That was not a compliment, just an observation. I was given some limited training... what to expect, how to react... but honestly... the training seemed hurried... they appeared to be rushed for time and needed to get this going... ASAP."

"Curious, I've been in here ten years and you arrived a year ago... that does not sound like they were in much of a rush to me."

"I agree."

"Were there others being trained to test... at the same time as you?"

"No, it was just me. I also thought that was a bit unusual. A project this big, one would think there would be hundreds of testers..."

"Yes, one would think..."

We finish our meal and it's time for me to head out and find a new place to stay. I decide to leave Kathy on a positive note... no use letting all of our past disagreements... and hostile attitudes prevent us from parting as friends. Frankly, I have quite enough enemies... and don't need any more.

As we leave the restaurant, I hold out my hand, "Thanks for nursing me back to health... I will never forget that. Good luck on your journeys... and I will make you this promise. If I am ever able to get out of this *Sim*... I will find out your status... and if you are still in here... I will personally come back and rescue you."

Improving the Situation

Apparently, this catches Kathy by surprise… she looks up at me… tears in her eyes, "I'm sorry I was such a bitch, James… I will miss you… and good luck." With that, we embrace… and for the first time in a long while, I feel my body coming back to life. I don't want to let her go but finally do. Kathy smiles, turns, and walks back toward the hotel. I watch as she retreats… out of my life… forever.

…

This is one of our larger *SimCity* and if memory serves, there should be a least a dozen hotels in the downtown area alone. Our goal was to accommodate a 100k guests per *SimCity* per day. I stroll around town, constantly looking for the emergency exit door, and also begin scanning for a hotel. Since I may be here another week… even several more weeks, I do want a nice place. Apparently, Kathy was not given the deluxe package… but I decided not to say anything about that… as I'm sure she was feeling bad enough… without me pouring any *Sim*-salt into her already inflamed wounds.

I look for a tower or round structure atop a tall building… and finally spot one… a few blocks away, and make my way in that direction. Fortunately, it is in the opposite direction of the Bates Motel… thank God for small favors.

I arrive, drop my *Keycard* on the counter, and request the best room available. "Sorry, sir, but we are all booked up at this time… there is a quaint little residential cottage down the street… maybe two blocks… I believe they have vacancies."

I stare at the desk clerk for half a minute... in disbelief. He blinks a few times but continues to return my stare. "Uh... if you will run my card... I am certain a room will show up in inventory," I decide to reply.

The desk clerk looks down at the card but does not touch it. "No need, sir, as I stated... we are fully booked... there is a large convention in town... will there be anything else?"

"Yes, there will be... I demand a room... call your manager now!"

"Yes, sir, one moment please." The desk clerk walks to the nearest *Comm* unit, "Manager Walsh to the front desk, please... Manager Walsh to the front desk."

"She will be here momentarily, sir. Have a nice day." The desk clerk leaves and begins sorting incoming mail and placing it into the various resident boxes. I am not so much mad... as I am bewildered. This is not a programmed situation... if they ran the card and then reacted, based on my established credit limit or package restrictions, then I would understand... but they simply looked at the card and then rejected me out of hand. That is not a valid program path.

It takes several minutes, but finally, the apparent manager arrives, "Good afternoon, sir, my name is Francine Walsh, but please call me Fran. How may I assist you today?"

I decide on the direct approach, "Please pickup my *Keycard* and insert it into your registration machine... over there... and then we will talk."

Fran looks at me, does not blink but after a few seconds delay, retrieves the *Keycard* from the desk, heads over to the registration machine, and inserts the card. The register glows a bright green... showing the highest level of acceptance. Fran retrieves the card, returns and places it on the counter in front of me. "Yes, Mr. Caldwell, what may I do for you today?"

"I thought that was obvious... I would like a room... a large suite with a view of downtown... please."

"As I am certain Mr. Phillips informed you, we are currently at capacity and have no rooms available. As a matter of fact, we are fully booked through next Thursday, that's when the convention leaves."

"What convention… there is no convention in town… there is no one in this city except for the *Sims*… what the fuck is going on here?" I am quickly losing patience, but even more importantly… I am becoming frightened.

"Sir, while I realize you are a VIP… I will not stand here and be cursed at. We have no rooms available… please take you card… and leave the hotel."

…

As I look at Fran, I notice several very large guys in uniform approaching. I turn to face them. "Is there trouble, Miss Walsh?" one of the uniformed attendants asks.

"No Bill, just a misunderstanding. Mr. Caldwell was just leaving, but please be so kind as to escort him to the main door… and thank you."

I look at Fran, and then at Bill. They stare at me, but do not move. I turn and head to the main door. They do not follow. I am out on the street and badly in need of a drink. What the fuck is going on here? I say to myself.

…

There is a bar down the street from the hotel… but then, there is always a bar down the street from the hotel, why would there not be? I head in and very few folks are there. It is almost 5PM and the place should be crowded. I take a seat at the bar, the bartender arrives, "Yes sir, what is your pleasure this evening?"

"Double scotch on the rocks… make it a Glenlivet." I drop my card onto the counter, she picks it up, winks, and heads over to pour the drink. I start to relax, ever so slightly.

"Here you are James. May I call you James?" she asks.

"Yes, and your name is?" I inquire, as the bartender places a wooden coaster on the table, and then slowly and methodically places the scotch glass on top of the coaster.

"I'm Betty… and how are you today?"

"Let me have a couple of sips of scotch before I answer that," I reply.

Betty smiles, turns and heads over to the glasses rack, and starts polishing the wine glasses. I pick up the scotch... wow, this is a heavy lead crystal double rocks glass... did not know we had these. I take a sip... smooth... I take a larger sip, and immediately begin to relax. Not sure what that last hotel experience was all about... that has never happened to me in the ten years I've been on this journey to find my way out of here.

I retrieve my *SmartComm* and begin taking notes to myself. I briefly describe my experience at the *Grand Hotel* and decide to make a footnote. 'Something is beginning to change. I have felt it for a while now, but until I arrived in this city... I was not certain. Now, I am becoming increasingly concerned and even a little frightened. What is happening? I am not sure... but there has been a shift... a reality shift if you will... and I must attempt to figure out what it is all about. However, my first priority continues to be my personal survival... and attempting to find a way out of this... madhouse. My secondary mission, which I am now adding to my log, is to ensure that Kathy Patterson, an employee of *FgU,* is also safely extracted... retrieved from this *Sim.* More on Kathy... later.'

After two scotches, I am quite relaxed. Given the lack of customers, Betty hangs around a lot... and I have no objection to that. "What brings you to town, James?" Betty asks.

I decide to pretend that Betty is real... and interact with her as I would any other gorgeous female... with the possible exception of Kathy.

"Just passing through," I respond.

"Are you a zombie fan... we have some of the best areas for zombie hunters... or even zombie huntees... if you get my drift."

I get her drift... there are some folks out there who actually like to be hunted, caught, and then slowly and painfully devoured by zombies, vampires, winged bats or whatever... who am I to judge. They pay their money and they get what they want... or need.

"No, I hate zombies… that was not why I came here… BTW, how long have you been bartending here… and what do you know about the *Grand Hotel*… down the street?" I decide to ask.

"Oh, I am an original… but do not keep track of actual time. I prefer to experience my pleasure on a day-to-day and moment-by-moment basis."

That is one of the 100-plus standard 'come on' lines, but, for now at least, I choose to ignore it. "And the hotel?"

"I keep out of their way and they keep out of mine… that's all I will say regarding … the *Grand Hotel.*"

"Is there a problem over there?" I fish.

"No problem… but in case you haven't noticed… they are always fully booked… but no one is ever in there. One would think that we would get hundreds of folks a week from over there… but, to my knowledge, I've never seen a soul who is staying there come in for a drink… conversation… lunch."

"Strange," I reflect.

"Odd," Betty replies.

Betty continues her flirting… but I decide to pass on having company tonight. She does suggest a quaint cottage (B&B) down the street, and right before dark, I head over there. They have several available rooms, I take one, and head to my room for the night. Fortunately, no zombies are out tonight… I must be in the better part of town.

Making a Decision

I sleep fine in the cottage; the bed is soft and comfy, just the way I like it. Breakfast is served in the main dining room… and as expected, I am eating alone. Their coffee is better than I've been getting lately, and then I remember Kathy. Maybe, even the *Sim*-coffee is cheaper in economy class. I had not even thought about that. I should, at least, get Kathy an upgrade before I leave this *STR*… it is the least I can do… after all she's done to me… I mean for me.

On my way out of the B&B, in order to continue my daily scouting venture, I stop by the front desk. "Nice room… so I will not be checking out, at least for a while. Now you have my *Keycard* on file, so if for some reason I fail to show up one morning, or one evening, for that matter, go ahead and just run the final bill… It will go through without issue."

"No problem, Mr. Caldwell… anything else I can do for you this morning?"

"Yes, there is one thing. I have a friend, who will be staying in town for quite a while… could be months or even years. She is in a cheaper hotel over on Marshall Street. Can you recommend a really first class hotel in the downtown area? She deserves a bit better accommodations… and some entertainment to boot. And, if possible, as far away from zombies and monsters as she can get."

"So, she's not interested in a B&B?"

"No, it's not for everyone. I believe she is looking for something a bit more upscale… maybe a large suite with a nice view of the river."

"Yes, I know just the place. I have a map… let's touch *SmartComms* and I'll transfer it for you. It's called *Duncan*

Imperial Suites and Resort. Most of the locals just call it the *Imperial Hotel.* This is the only place in town that offers tennis, golf, nine holes only; a large pool, several bars… pretty much everything one would ask for… but I must warn you… it is top dollar. Platinum level, maybe even Plat-Plus. And, if you stick to the well-lit streets in the area… there will be no zombies."

"Perfect. Can you do me one additional favor? Will you call over there and make a reservation in the name of Kathy Peterson? Go ahead and secure the room deposit using my *Keycard*… I authorize that now." I hand my *Keycard* back to the desk clerk, he runs it… I press the 'Accept' button, imprint my thumb… and we are all set. "Thanks! I appreciate the extra service," I reply as I leave the B&B and head out to scout the town… looking for any clues that may assist me in escaping from my self-created worst nightmare.

…

I decide to head in the direction of the *Imperial Hotel,* check it out, then head over to Kathy's and tell her what I've located. Now, I don't expect her to be grateful, I'm not certain she possesses the gratitude gene (maybe I could install a chip?). But at least that will be something nice I can do for a fellow traveler…

It is noon before I reach the hotel, since I am in no real hurry… and stop in several shops, and generally get the lay of the land. As I walk into the hotel, I think to myself, "Now, this will work. It is exactly what I was looking for yesterday, when I, unfortunately, stumbled into the *Grand Hotel.* The place is plush… top shelf. Lots of dark wood, huge windows looking out over the massive pool, hot tub… and spa area.

I decide to head to the front desk and make sure my reservations are confirmed… before I head over and talk to Kathy. "Yes, Mr. Caldwell. Bill, over at the B&B, called and we have the perfect room for your friend. Top floor… full view of the river… huge lanai… and it even comes with daily butler service, at no extra charge. The rate is all inclusive… there is a fully stocked liquor cabinet, and a fresh bottle of her choice of wine or champagne is delivered each evening at exactly 5PM. Since you have an unlimited spending limit, being an owner and all, I won't even bore you with the price… unless you want to know… just for your accounting purposes."

"Yes, I would like to know in round numbers," I reply, just curious what the best costs… these days.

"Now, the daily rate is $2200 credits, but we've got her in at a monthly rate which is quite favorable. Let's see, yes, that nets to $35,000 a month… on a month-to-month basis… prorated to the next half month."

"That is fine, anything else I need to do to ensure she gets that room for as long as she likes… even for the rest of her life if that is what it takes."

"No, sir, you are all set. We would love to have her as a permanent resident… we have weekly parties, and lots of other activities, chaperone services, of course… I'll personally assure she has a full list of services. I assume you want the 'unlimited package'."

"Yes, the unlimited package will do just fine." I hand him my *Keycard* and authorize the first six months… in advance.

I leave the *Imperial* feeling pretty damn good about myself. Finally, I did something for someone else… performed an unselfish act. "How long has it been since I've done that?" I ask myself…. "Too damn long," I reply.

I decide to head back to Kathy's hotel, get her packed and out of that dump as soon as possible. It would be a shame if I *Reset* before I told her the good news… so I hustle on over, head directly to her room, and knock on her door.

…

No answer. I knock several more times but still no answer. I head downstairs and look in the common area… out in the small garden… no luck.

Okay, I guess I'll check in later in the day, she could, of course, be out… but at the last minute, I decide to ask at the front desk. "I'm looking for Kathy Peterson, room 1608… I knocked but no one answered."

"Yes, I saw Ms. Peterson this morning at 8:43AM, she was heading out of the breakfast café, and took the elevator back to her floor. She has not come back down since or I would have seen her... I never leave the desk."

"Okay, maybe I'll go back up and knock some more."

"Why don't just use you key, Mr. Caldwell? It is still active. She has not yet deactivated your access."

"Are you sure that is okay?"

"Sure, she came down yesterday and we discussed changing the access, but at the last minute, she decided against it. She seemed rather sad... depressed... and I was a little concerned."

"Okay, I'll go back up and try again. Thanks for your help."

I return to the elevator, press 16 and head back to her room. Once again, I knock, louder this time... no response. I decide to use my key and enter. Fortunately, I forgot to give it back to her once I departed yesterday.

"Kathy... it's James... are you in there? ...sorry to barge in but I have some very good news..." I stop, dead in my tracks... there is Kathy on the floor... lying in a pool of blood.

Owning My Responsibilities

I run over to Kathy, kneel beside her, and take her pulse. It takes a moment to find it... but she is still alive. Her left arm has been badly cut... but the bleeding appears to have stopped. I look at the floor... less than a liter of blood loss... so she may be okay. I have to decide if I need to get others involved... but quickly conclude that I need to handle this, by myself. The time for passing the buck... is over.

...

Kathy remains unconscious for several hours. I do not move her but find a few blankets to cover her, in an attempt to keep her warm. I do not have a thermometer, but she feels cold and her skin is clammy. I do attempt to clean up the wound... but before I can complete that task, the wound begins once again seeping blood. I run to the kitchenette, grab a hand towel, return, and wrap it around her arm. That appears to stop the bleeding for now. I look around for alcohol... not to drink, but to sanitize the wound and prevent possible infection. I spot a bottle of gin. It remains sealed. I open it and liberally pour the gin over the hand towel and into the wound. Apparently, that stings... and Kathy twitches her arm slightly.

Needing her to continue to rest, I cease the antiseptic process and slowly move her arm down beside her, parallel with the rest of her body. She appears to head back into slumber, so I slowly move away, pull up one of the small side chairs... and wait it out.

It is another hour before I hear her begin to moan, softly at first, but then the volume increases. I am kneeling beside her in a moment and take hold of her right hand. Her moaning ceases and she returns to sleep. After a few minutes, I let go of her hand and start to return to my chair, but the moaning immediately returns, so I decide just to kneel there and continue holding her hand.

Finally, after a total of over four hours, Kathy begins to awaken. I am right there, holding her hand, when at first, one eye blinks, and then opens slightly. She mumbles something, but I can't make out the words. She does, however, squeeze my hand and I take that as a positive sign.

It takes several more minutes, but she next moves her right hand, taking a firm grip on my hand... and the second eyes blinks a couple of time and then opens. "James..."

"Yes, Kathy, I am here. Don't worry about a thing... you are going to be fine," I state in as positive a tone as I can muster.

"Oh, shit... I was afraid of that," she replies... and slowly releases her grip on my hand. I realize that once Kathy is awake, I will need to force fluids in to her... a lot of fluids... and not the alcohol kind. I take the opportunity to run back over to the kitchen, find a tall glass, put in one ice cube, and fill it with water. I do not see any straws... but then why would there be straws? I dump about a third of the water out of the glass... and return to Kathy's side.

Kathy remains in her current semi-conscience state for another thirty or so minutes, but then begins to move her head, looking toward me. "Can I get some water... my mouth is very dry?" she asks.

"Of course... it's right here... but sip slowly... no need to rush."

Kathy takes a couple of sips, coughs, and then, "Oh God, that hurt. My left arm... ohhh, I really fucked up this time."

"Do you have any *Sim*-ASP or other pain relievers?" I ask.

"Yes... over there in the first drawer... on the left."

I head back over, retrieve four ASP, and return. "Here, take these... your pain is likely to increase over the next few hours... but, assuming no infection, it should start to feel better after that."

"And what makes you the expert on pain?" Kathy asks.

"Oh, I thought that was obvious… I've been in this hell-hole for ten years… and unfortunately… many times, I actually survived the monster attacks. On those occasions, I don't get the luxury of resetting and starting over… but had to live with the pain until either I healed… or I eventually, died."

"Sorry, I asked," Kathy replies, and she can barely speak.

"Let's try more water… but slowly?"

"I get it, James… slow…" I have to note, just for the record, I guess… that even when near death… Kathy remains a royal bitch.

···

It is another hour before Kathy is able to sit up. Fortunately, the bleeding does not return… and I note no swelling or extreme redness (other than the ugly gashes up and down her left wrist). I use a pillow to prop her up against the side of the couch… we are not quite ready to try and stand.

"Do they have room service in this hotel?" I ask.

"What? Where do you think you are… the Waldorf Astoria? No room service… no restaurant… no bar…but hey, at least the rooms are small… that's gotta account for something, right?"

For some unknown reason, I find that last exchange to be… rather funny. Kathy is keen on the sarcasm… that is for sure. Maybe I need to rethink my negative reaction to virtually every breath she takes… since it appears that we may be together for quite a while.

"Okay, but you need something to eat… something liquid… like chicken soup…"

"Oh, yea… *Sim*-Chicken soup… one of my all-time favs."

"Then what would you like to eat, Kathy?" I respond, in a soft and hopefully caring-sounding voice.

"Go check the fridge over there… I bought some high energy drinks the other day…."

I head to the fridge, and yes, I spot them, dump one in to a glass and return to Kathy. "Here, drink this."

Kathy drinks… and does not cough. It takes a couple of minutes, but she is finally able to drink the entire glass of *HiEnrgX*.

"Is there anything else I can get you, at the moment, Kathy?" I ask.

"Yes, a new life would be great… thanks!" I resist the urge…

Finally, Kathy is ready to transition over to the bed. I help her to stand, and we slowly walk over. I place her gently down on the bed, and she is able to roll in, on her own, without hitting her left arm. "Thanks, James… maybe I'll take a short nap, but please… don't leave."

"I'm not going anywhere, Kathy."

…

It is several more hours before Kathy awakens. I do not leave the hotel room. Fortunately, I find almost a half-bottle of wine in the refrigerator… and I decide to have that as my reward for being such a good Samaritan (i.e. much less of an ass-hole than usual).

"Can I get a few more ASPs please… my arm is killing me?" Kathy squeaks, barely audible. I retrieve the pills and refresh her water glass.

"Thanks James."

"NP."

Recovery

It has now been over eighteen hours since I found Kathy lying, bleeding on the floor, close to death. She awakes for a while... asks for a few things... and then returns to sleep. She seems to be improving... but it's still much too early to tell. It will probably be several days before she is ready to get 'up and about'. That's fine... I will be patient... and be there if and when she needs me.

...

It is on the third day that Kathy gets out of bed for the first time. She has begun eating solid food, some shit I found in her fridge... Vegan Meat Loaf? Really? "I need to take a shower," she announces. I know better than to offer her any help... she's already basically accused me of trying to get...

"Aren't you going to help me?" she asks, in her new and certainly not improved, gravelly voice.

"Sure... what can I do to assist?"

"Just help me into the bathroom... I'll take care of the rest."

I'm sure you will... I think to myself, but say nothing... out loud. I hear the water running, and take the opportunity to get myself something to munch on. It's been days since I've eaten anything substantial, but she still has a few *Sim*-Cheese sticks left, so I devour those... and chase it down with water (the wine ran out yesterday... and I've not been able to go out to get more... damn it!)

...

"Are you asleep?" I hear a voice but cannot quite place it… oh, yea, now I remember…

"Just nodded off for a moment… did you need something?" I state, rather groggily.

"No, I'm better… the pain has stopped and my left arm seems to be healing… faster than I had expected."

"That's VR for you… everything inside the *Sim* is accelerated…"

"Can we talk?" Kathy asks as she sits next to me on the couch.

"Sure, Kathy… if you want… but let me say this before you start… you do not owe me an explanation… on anything… understand?"

"Yes, I understand… but we still need to talk."

"Okay, but, if this is going to be a serious discussion, I would sure like a drink in my hand… if you feel up to going out… maybe to that bar down the street?"

"Yes, I believe I may be up for that… and we can get a real meal, while we are there."

…

I do help Kathy, but only to the extent of holding her hand while we walk… and attempt to walk a bit slower than usual. We make it to the bar in just a few minutes, and decide to sit at a high top slightly away from the main bar.

"I'll have a glass of white wine," Kathy states, weakly.

"Scotch for me, double… Glenlivet," I respond.

The drinks arrive and we sip them… but say very little for a few minutes.

"I guess you want an explanation?" Kathy begins.

"No, I do not need an explanation, Kathy. We each make decisions that we have to live with… or die with as the case may be. Do you think that in the last ten years, I have never thought of suicide… as a way out of this nightmare?"

"And what did you do about those thoughts?"

"If you really want to know, I'll tell you. But, as you know… I am not a 'Yes' or 'No' guy… so do you want me to tell you or remain quiet?"

"Sorry, I've been so rude in the past. Tell me your story… I promise to listen and not to criticize."

I begin with my second year here on Fantasy Island (sorry… but we did steal a few ideas from that show, as well). I had been doing everything humanly possible to find a way out of this madhouse… or maze as I called it back then. I assumed it was all a puzzle, and all I had to do was to solve the puzzle and I would be freed… and returned to my life.

"The realization finally came to me that I would not be returning to my life or my love… but really might be trapped here for all of eternity. I became serious depressed, and finally, decided it was time to end it all."

"What did you do?" Kathy asks,

"Fought it off for as long as I could… but finally, it took control over me and I knew I had to try to end it all."

I stop, take a sip of scotch, and then continue, "So one day I decided to see if it was possible to commit suicide. I mean, I had already been killed and devoured dozens of times… and I had always been *Reset*… and had to start over. But, somewhere in my mind I felt that if I initiated the action… and killed myself… then the nightmare would be over."

"Well, obviously that did not work," Kathy announces.

"Duh… you think… and here I thought you were going to let me tell my story… without interruptions… I should have known better!"

"Sorry… but the ending was so obvious… where was the suspense…? I see you sitting here… next to me, even smiling, at times, and so… I just… surmised… sorry I spoiled the big ending."

It's time for another deep breath… boy I sure have been doing a lot of that lately. "Yes, Kathy, I failed… but there was a point to the story…"

"I know, James, the point was to never give up hope… keep trying… look for a better tomorrow."

Actually, that wasn't the point at all, but I like that much better than my original point, "Yes… but it would have been nice if you had allowed me to express that point… since it was my story."

"Okay, sorry… I have a tendency to complete other people's sentences for them…"

"Duh… I would never have even considered that…"

"Okay, crawl down off your high horse," Kathy states.

"Why?" I reply.

Kathy gets up from her seat and comes toward me… not sure if I should duck or run screaming out of the bar. But as I look up at her… she places her right hand against my cheek… pulls me close… and kisses me… on the cheek. "Thank you, James, for saving my life. I understand what you did and I appreciate it. Maybe not at first… but now… thank you."

I am, of course, stunned… and at a loss for words (now, don't go there). It takes a few moments to recover… and I must admit, finishing my double scotch is a part of those moments.

It is my turn to capitulate, admit my shortcomings, "I am sorry that I, basically, walked out on you… leaving you to who-knows-what."

"All is forgiven, James, I do understand my strong suits, and my weaknesses… but just understanding them does not change them. Yes, I was pissed at you for causing all of my suffering this last year… and that was wrong. Thanks for forgiving me."

"I don't believe I actually said I'd forgiven you," I state, but attempt a small and noticeable smile, "But let's go with that for now."

…

We eat… and food never tasted so good. After a week of left-over vegan meat-loaf… it was good to be back into the real-world. Well, I guess that was a bit of an overstatement… since this is certainly not the real world.

Resolution

As we leave the bar and begin to head back to the hotel, it is time to spring the news, "What did you bring with you... when you came on this Beta test assignment?" I ask.

"Bring... you can't bring anything with you... that is *there* and this is *here*..."

"Wow... I've never heard it expressed that eloquently before... but I guess what I meant was... what is back at the hotel that you want to keep... take with you?"

"Take with me... are we going somewhere? Just because I kissed you back there... that is no reason to assume..."

"I assume nothing" I stop, look at Kathy, and then, "Is there anything in the hotel that you would take with you... if and when you decide to leave?"

"No!"

"Good, then follow me," I state, as I take her hand and we head, rapidly, toward the *Imperial Hotel.*

...

We arrive in the lobby of the *Imperial,* I glance at Kathy, and she is taking in the ambiance. "I saw this place when I first arrived... they did not accept my card... told me to look elsewhere for 'lodging'."

"Life changes, Kathy, even virtual life," I state as we walk up to the front desk.

"Welcome back, Mr. Caldwell," the desk clerk states, and he is smiling.

"This must be the lovely lady whose room is prepared and waiting for her."

"What does he mean?" Kathy states as she looks over at me, questioningly.

"Let's just go with it… and see where that leads," I respond.

The desk clerk hands Kathy a key and states… twenty-fifth floor… best view in town… enjoy."

Kathy accepts the key but looks at me. I take her hand and we head for the elevator. Before we can leave the front desk, the clerk states. "Excuse me, Mr. Caldwell but the Penthouse elevator is over there… that one is for our… regular guests."

We head in the direction the clerk indicates, and we see the elevator, which has a small sign, stating 'Penthouse Only'. As we approach, the door opens and we enter. The door closes, but there are no buttons to push. We feel the elevator leave the ground floor… and in seconds it stops, and the door opens.

"Kathy Peterson… we hope you to have a wonderful stay and anything we can do to make that stay more enjoyable… please let us know." The door closes and we walk to the very first room… uh… apparently the only room on this floor.

"What the fuck is this James?" Kathy asks.

"Let's go in and find out," I state… really beginning to enjoy this experience.

As Kathy approaches the door, it disappears, and she is inside her suite. "Holy shit… what is this?" she asks as we enter the foyer… leading to the living room… and other parts of the suite.

"I just thought you might like an upgrade… after all of the hardship you've been through this last year, so I was able to acquire… a better situation," I state.

We enter the suite… which is actually, a large mansion… it has everything one could imagine… multiple bedrooms, each with its own private bath, a living room, formal dining area, large full kitchen, and a den. The den opens to the lanai.

"So, are we staying here tonight?" Kathy asks, obviously overwhelmed.

"You are staying here, Kathy, for as long as you remain in this *Sim*. This is your suite… everything is yours and cannot be taken away from you."

"I don't understand, James… why?"

"I created this monster... as you've aptly called it... Madhouse, I believe was another term you used. I want to make it up to you... I may not be able to get you out of this *Sim*, but at least I can make your life here... better than it was before."

We end the tour... I, too, am impressed. In my ten years here, I've never encountered a hotel anywhere remotely as upscale, luxurious... or swanky as this one.

Kathy locates the wet bar and quickly move toward it... "The booze... is that included?"

"Everything is included... all meals, drinks... everything... there are tennis courts, golf, exercise... spas... all of it. There is nothing you have to purchase... for as long as you are here, Kathy. I apologize for getting you into this... mess... and while I am unable to get you out... at least I can make your life a bit more pleasant... and tolerable."

Kathy takes a seat on the plush couch, lowers her head, and begins to cry. I did not see that coming. I walk over, take the seat next to her, and take her hand. She sobs for a minute, or maybe two.

"Are you okay?" I ask.

"I am wonderful... thanks to you. I can't believe this place..."

There is a knock on the door, 'Room Service'. Kathy gets up, runs to the door.

"Daily wine and Champagne service... what would you like? And here are some hors d'oeuvres for you to snack on."

The attendant wheels in a large cart, and begins to unload food, wine, Champagne. As I look over at Kathy, she is smiling, and looks back at me with appreciation and gratitude. But, her smile quickly turns into a frown, as I begin to dissolve... "No!" she shouts, but it is too late... I am *Reset.*

The Horror Show

I awake back at the castle. It is a different castle, of course. They are all somewhat different. There are subtle changes, and sometimes, even major, significant changes. I never know until I arrive and attempt to make my way through… and then on to the *City* (assuming I get that far without dying or being otherwise indisposed… or is it decomposed…). While I am somewhat depressed over having to leave Kathy… I am certainly glad I was able to improve her life before I left. At least I can feel good about that… as I press forward on my personal quest to find my way out of this trap, and back home.

This castle is even more sinister-looking and feeling than the Bentley Castle. It is more gothic, with tall pointy roof lines... probably security towers… one never knows. Not sure if this one has a name… just hope I live long enough to find out. I, once again, briefly think of Kathy. I hope we meet again, someday. The odds of that happening are small… but not impossible. I've reset in the exact same place and in the same *STR* on several occasions… but the chances are very slim that both the place and time will be exactly the same as when I met Kathy; most likely not.

I feel their eyes upon me but cannot yet see them. I detect multiple beings… humanoids… not mechanical or androidic this time. Of course, I arrive at the staircase and must make my first, and possibly, my last decision. Since last time I went up… this time I choose down. As I slowly and silently descend the stairway, the torch lights begin to fade. I retrieve my *SmartComm*, press the torch button, and… the light flickers on, but is noticeably weaker than before. These LCDs will not last much longer.

I reach the dungeon level, and decide, this time, to try a maneuver I have not used in a while, and when I have employed it… it has always failed.

I run like hell.

I take the shortest path through the dungeon level. I am on a slight but steady incline… constantly moving upward toward ground level. There are winding turns, and several obstacles along the way. I wish I could turn off the torch but it is pitch dark down here and I cannot see even five feet ahead. I make it through the torture chambers and arrive at the several hangman stations. I see several dead and decayed bodies still swinging from their hangman noose.

I quickly turn right, exit the chamber and arrive in the administration portion of the dungeon. Since this section has some dim lighting, I douse my torch and quickly stow my *SmartComm*. I still can't see today's monsters but I can feel them… they are catching up… and being cautiously quiet in the process. I see four bright green eyes directly ahead… possibly preventing me from continuing my trek forward. I've seen this trick before, however, so do not slow or change direction, allowing the monsters to catch me. Instead, I run directly into and through the illusional four green eyes… and I am out of the castle dungeon into the partial sunlight.

Almost home… I begin a full sprint, up the hill and through the graveyard. The *City* should be on the other side of that hill… but I am never quite certain what I will find. As I approach the graves, I begin hearing the moans… screams… pleading of those encased within their assigned tombs but wanting out. And, out they come. As the ghosts, ghouls, and goblins begin their slow climb out of their individual resting places, I begin dodging them. I trip and a ghoul is on me, bloody fangs biting the flesh of my lower right leg. I pick it up by the hair on its head, look it directly in its bloodshot eyes, and quickly shove it away from me. I'm back on my feet, but limping, my leg now hurts like hell. This slows me down but I am determined not to allow my pain to impede my progress.

Several monsters are heading in my direction, I feign right and then charge left toward the clearing ahead. One catches me by his fingernails; I hear my shirt tear and feel the pain as his nails scrape across the bare skin of my arm. One more ahead, so I jump, left foot up high, and kick it squarely in the face, I feel the blood splatter across my body as its head rolls onto the ground.

I am through the graveyard and see the ridge ahead. As I top it, I look below... there is the *City*. Looks to be 1890ish... possibly London, England... hard to tell with all of the fog covering most of the landscape below. I decide not to look back, but see the trail down, and begin descending the cliff. I am about halfway down when my damaged leg decides it's had enough, buckles, and I fall. I tumble and slide the remainder of the way to the bottom and end up knee deep in a dirty, damp, and rather disgusting swamp.

At least I am alive and for the moment, safe. It is daylight; I am in sight of the *City*... and unless the rules have changed, once again, I should be okay as long as I find accommodations before dark. Unfortunately, between the bites, the scratches, and the damage caused by my tumble half-way down that sizeable cliff, I am in no condition to walk, so decide just to remain where I am, in the swamp, until I am able to regain my strength.

Looking Forward... Never Back

It takes a while, but finally, I am able to get myself out of the swamp and begin the walk toward town. On the plus side, the city appears to be less than a mile away. On the negative side, I have stabbing pains throughout most of my body. Nothing life-threatening... assuming this *STR* does not also have that 'infection enhancement'. Then all bets are off.

I spot a small house as I make my way toward the outskirts of the city. I knock on the door, and a young boy, maybe twelve, answers. "Can you help me, please?" I ask. "Do you have any alcohol or anything I can use to put on these wounds?"

"Sure, but you'll have to wait out here. My mom does not allow strangers in our home."

"Good for your mother... I'll sit out here at that bench... thank you."

The boy is gone for several minutes, but finally returns. "I brought several things from the medicine cabinet... here... use what you need."

"Thank you son, my name is James, what's yours?" I ask.

"Ben. Sounds like you were messing around at the castle or maybe even the graveyard... I thought adults knew better than to go up there?"

"They should... guess I'm rather stupid," I reply. I see peroxide and several other *Sim* products, and apply them to my wounds. I spot a couple of large Band-aids... and a small strip of cloth I can use for a bandage.

"Sorry, we don't have any extra food... but times have been pretty tough lately. Mom has to work twelve hours every day just to make ends meet. Sorry I can't offer more."

"This is great… and I appreciate your help." It takes me the better part of an hour, but finally, I am all patched up and ready to go. "Thank you so much for your help, Ben." I reach in my pocket, pull out a twenty pound note, and hand it to Ben. "Give this to your mom… it should help."

"Gee, thank you, sir… that's more money than she earns in a month… downtown."

"You are a good kid… your mom is lucky to have you," I state as my parting words. I stand, take a deep breath, and head for the *City*. I leave Ben, looking at the note… somewhat in disbelief.

I remain in pain but do not seem to be getting an infection, so assume I'll be okay by tomorrow. Most virtual bites, scrapes and bruises are gone by the next day. The game designers figured that one day of pain and agony was enough to endure.

I continue toward the *City*, see a hotel up ahead and head for it. "Sure, we have rooms available, Mr. Caldwell, the desk clerk responds once I hand him my *Keycard*. Even in 1890 London, my *Keycard* is welcome… how special is that.

"Where can I get a drink?" I ask.

"If you head down the street, you'll see Fred's Place on the right. They have a half price on pints going on right now." I decide to head up to my room first; I take a bath (no showers in 1890 London… not in this *Sim* anyway). I soak in the tub for over an hour. The desk clerks sends a 'girl' up to pour the hot water, but we never make eye contact. She does her job, I tip her a pound note, and she leaves. Yes, that is a huge tip for 1890, but then, I believe in large tips… they usually end up paying for themselves over time.

Once I am dressed (the 'girl' brought some clothes… another pound tip… she may be able to buy her own home… soon), I am on my way down to visit Fred. Now, just to keep the record straight… it's not so much that I want to drink all of the time… which I do… but bars are the best place in town to communicate… find out what is going on… and that is always my primary mission once I arrive at a new *SimCity*.

I am stiff, but the pain has already begun to recede, and once I arrive at Fred's, I am feeling much better. "What for you, stranger?" the bar keep asks.

"Gimme a pint of your most popular draft beer. Do you have chilled glasses?" I inquire (everyone knows the English like their beer warm... yuk!).

"Sure, we keep a couple of chilled mugs for our out-of-town quests... where you from and is this your first visit to London?" the barkeep inquires.

"Yes and yes," I reply. "I'm from the US. Just got in on the... boat... should be here for the next few weeks. Can I open an account... prepay for everything?"

"Certainly, you can. You will find us English folk quite accommodating... and very friendly."

I place my *Keycard* on the table, the barkeep picks it up, winks, and runs it through the same automated credit machine they use in every *SimCity* in this...

Game. I need to continue to remind myself... this is a *Game* and not reality.

Basically, I hate beer. Any beer and all beers. I am a wine and scotch guy basically, but I don't believe they have any wine in 1890 London... but Scotch?

"Can I get a scotch instead?" I ask once the barkeep returns my card.

"Yes, sir... you can have pretty much anything you want... I've got the good stuff in the back... I'll be right back." The barkeep heads to the back room and returns with a fully-sealed bottle. "This one is all yours, I'll keep it on this shelf for whenever you want it... and don't worry... no one will touch it... if they want to keep their hand." He smiles, breaks the seal, and pours a double... neat.

"Since I'm from the States... could I have an ice cube or two?" I ask.

"Certainly, sir, we have ice... I'll be right back." He leaves once again but returns, with a small glass filled with ice. "Whatever your heart desires... just let me know... I have friends... we can get you anything that is legal... and most things that aren't."

I sip my scotch and finally relax. Scotch helps with the pain... everyone know that... both physical and psychological pain. After a couple of refreshers, I ask Fred, the barkeep and owner, "I'm currently staying at the hotel down the street, is that a good one... or can I do better?"

"Oh, they are good. Maybe not be the best hotel in town... but they are the most accommodating... that's the specialty in this area of London... we *accommodate*!" Not exactly sure what all that means... but it seems I've selected well, so decide to settle in and make this section of London my home... until further notice.

Searching for Clues

Over the next week, Fred and I become great friends. Yes, he's the owner and the barkeep. He is always there... from the time the pub opens at 11AM until they close at midnight. He gives me leads on good places to eat... and good people to meet. Now, one of the primary reasons to create an entertainment *Sim* is... *socialization*... everyone knows that... let's be real here. Yes, we want to eat and be eaten by zombies, but we also want to eat and be eaten by... well, let's not get into the crude details... we all understand the scope of 'entertainment'.

My hotel room is adequate for the occasion, and the services I receive are much better than average. I really do not go in for virtual sex... even though there is no noticeable difference between real and virtual sex. To me, sex is part of a love package. I won't tell you I've never had a one-night stand... but I prefer to be in love... if I am going to have sex with someone. Call me old-fashioned.

...

After triangulating my *SmartComm* via several points within the *City*, the *STR* is calculated to be 1889 London, early spring... late March or early April. I've been in London for two weeks, but I've gotten not a single clue as to where there might be a hidden escape hatch. Now after ten years, you may be wondering... is there really such a thing as an escape hatch... or exit door?

Well, all I can tell you is this. As part of the *Sim* package I created... every single city has at least one exit door. These were to be used when, for example, inside-game maintenance was required in a *Sim*. The workman could come in through the usual portal... fix the problem, and then exit via the escape hatch.

Now, unfortunately, when I decided to take my final Beta test before declaring the *Sim* 'open for business', I did not think it was necessary to carry the list of all Exit doors with me... my bad.

...

I awake from a restful sleep. Why you don't dream in *Sim,* I have no idea. Everything else seems to function normally.

It is 6:15AM and I usually awake more like 8AM. But, I decide to get up and head downstairs for coffee and breakfast. While I have never been a fan of 'English Food', I enjoy the breakfast... the pastries... all of it. Since you cannot gain or lose weight in Sim, I really do not need to watch what I eat... but do need to exercise. Within the *Sim*, the muscles seem to respond better to exercise... I'm not really sure why.

...

During my travels this day, I pick up a local paper and stop in at Fred's for a scotch and read the paper. It may be a *Sim*, but we attempt to keep everything in some semblance of space-time context. For example, If I went back to 1969 Earth, USA, in July... there would be a great deal of news about Neil Armstrong landing on the moon... but there would not be any actual moon rides... since that does not happen until somewhere around 2050. That's what I mean by 'context'. We attempt to make the selected period/place as authentic as is possible, reasonable, and financially feasible.

With scotch in hand, I check the headlines. Apparently, Jack the Ripper struck again last night. This is the first I've heard of Jack, since I've been here, so spend the next hour sipping my drink, and reading. According to the paper, this is his fifth victim, all female, all young and single. Now, to be quite honest, the *Sim*-World is programmed to support a great deal of violence; because that is what the folks who pay for the adventure want to see, enjoy, and experience. But that violence is limited to 'non-human', aliens and animatronics, including robots, animated characters, and androids. Jack the Ripper... was real... horrible... and we *did not* program that 'feature' into any *Sim* scenario I've ever seen... or authorized.

Traffic is light this time of day, as most 'respectable' folks are working... and not sitting in some bar drinking... before noon. "Fred," I ask the next time he walks by and begins polishing the glasses (a sure sign of boredom), "what's going on with this 'Jack the ripper' fellow?" I inquire.

"That's right, Jim, you are not from around here... well it's the strangest thing... it all started last fall... at least once a month, a young, single and usually good-looking prostitute is killed... usually knifed, throat cut, and often ripped apart... mutilated... so the press began calling the damn murderer 'Jack the Ripper'. The official term is actually 'the Whitechapel Murderer'. Oh, no, did he strike again...? I have not looked at today's paper... been too busy."

"Yes, apparently... so why can't they find the bastard... and hang him from the nearest tree?"

"Oh, when they finally catch him... they will... he will never make it to trial... that's for sure."

"Any clues?" I ask, knowing that if anyone in this town knows anything... Fred is that 'anyone'.

"Uh, no... only what I read in the papers," and with that remark, Fred slowly turns away and heads back to polishing the glasses. That is so unlike Fred; even if he doesn't know much about any specific subject... he usually has a good tale to tell... maybe something he did... similar... in his youth. You can always count on Fred for a good story. I decide to let it pass and complete the article.

After putting down the paper, I become quite concerned. The method 'Jack' uses to torture and then kill his victims is nothing we would condone or allow inside our *Sim* environment. These are brutal attacks... there is no sport or gaming adventure value in simply killing prostitutes and then mutilating their bodies.

Since Fred is of no help here, I decide to talk to the local constable, head over to the local station house… and walk up to the desk where a sergeant is sitting behind a counter… reading the newspaper.

"May I help you, lad?" he states as he neatly folds the paper and puts it away.

"Yes, I arrived in London just a fortnight ago, and well, I read this morning about 'Jack the Ripper' and was wondering…

Well, obviously, that was the wrong thing to say. Within seconds, billy clubs are flying and I am being beaten to the ground. I offer no resistance, and am literally dragged into a holding cell, barely thirty feet from the Sergeant's desk.

Once the cage is locked, I get up off the floor and sit on one of the four cots in the room. The rooms stinks, of age, musk, dust, and decay. So much for realistic effects… maybe too much realism is not necessarily a good thing.

It is not long before a middle-aged gentleman, dressed to the tee in 1890 fashion, arrives, and pulls up a stool… outside of the jail cell. "So, you want to know about Jack the ripper, do ya?" he asks… in the best British cockney accent I've ever heard… I will have to congratulate the linguist… if I'm ever allowed to actually meet one.

"Yes, sir… I just wanted some information… as I said I'm just in from America… read that he had killed once again… and wanted to know if there was anything I could do to help catch him… and fry the bastard." I am attempting to work on my communication skills… how'd I do?

"So, you are from America, are ya… and you think you can catch this bastard, as you call him... while Scotland Yard cannot… is that your story?"

Those skills definitely do need more work. "No, sir… I just wanted to offer my help in catching him… given the fact that…" but I decide I've said enough.

"Given what fact, and why are you talking like that… are you a lawyer… Is that it… or are you after the bounty?"

"What bounty… I did not know there wa a reward for capturing him?'

"Yes, a hundred pounds… dead or alive… hopefully dead."

I wisely decide not to go into the 'fair trial' discussion, that is so 20th century US... and not 19th century England. "Okay, so I want to sign up to help... and possibly get the reward." Let's try that strategy on for size.

Things begin moving back in the right direction... less beatings and more begging. "Sorry, I pissed off the sergeant," I start.

"There you go again... what kinda word is 'pissed-off'? ...Okay, well, you must really be from America... they all talk funny over there... Let me see some ID, and then I will see if I can get you released..."

Since the only ID I have is my *Keycard*, I take it out and hand it to him. It does have my name, my photo, and my unlimited spending limit account number. "What is this? So you have no ID?"

"That is my ID... Oh, it's the new type, just issued in America... I'm sure it will get over here... shortly."

He looks at the card, hands it back. "Okay, you can go... but in the future... don't be coming into the police station and bothering the sergeant... he's much too busy... and gets riled up rather quickly."

...

I am back out on the street within the hour, battered, beaten... but never broken.

Rethinking my Involvement

On my way back to the hotel, as I metaphorically lick my wounds, I decide that just maybe I should stay out of the local town affairs. After all, I'm just passing through on my way to… who knows where. Best use my time finding clues and looking for the trap door… and leave the killers to the local police.

I spend the remainder of the day in my hotel. The beating has left me rather shaken, but I am certain that, by tomorrow morning, I will be my old self once again.

I do go out for a brief dinner… Sheppard's Pie… not my first choice… but… when in Rome… I have a couple of scotches, but decide to end my day early… and head quickly back to my hotel room.

…

I am doing better by the next morning, the bruises are beginning to heal and the pain is gone… overnight cures… one of my better design efforts. I decide to head back to Fred's… not even going to bring up the 'Jack' thing… but I am running low on information and need a few new avenues to explore before my next *Reset* occurs.

For the first time since coming to this bar, Fred is not there, "What for you lad?" the bartender asks as he wipes down the counter in front of me.

"Where is Fred?" I ask.

"Oh, he is not feeling well and is taking a few days off."

"Scotch, please," I state.

The bartender moves toward the standard swill, "No, Fred has the good stuff… reserved for me… it is right over…" I look over, but the bottle is not there. There was a half-bottle yesterday.

"Sorry, bud, but this is what we have… take it or leave it."

I think for a second, then decide, "Sorry, I forgot to give you my *Keycard*," I throw the card out onto the table, the bartender looks at It, but does not pick it up. "I don't know what that is… we take the currency of the Realm…. Nothing more… nothing less."

Nothing left to see here folks, I think to myself as I leave Fred's. Something has changed…. Or maybe I just need to wait a few days for Fred to return.

Not really having an agenda, and now becoming increasingly bored with 1890 London, I am content just to walk the streets. It is now late afternoon, and the fog begins to roll in, making everything appear surreal… even spooky. I decide to head back to the hotel, but as I turn, I look into the alley ahead… and spot her… standing there looking at me.

Not really being into prostitutes, either real or *Sim*, I turn away from her and begin my slow walk back to the hotel. "Excuse me, kind sir," I hear a soft female voice coming from behind me. I stop, turn and I am starring at possibly the most gorgeous female I'm seen since I arrived in this *Sim*.

I reach into my pocket, find a one pound note, and hand it to her, "Here buy some food… whatever you want… have a good day." I start to leave but she grabs my hand, "please don't go. Of course, I need the money, but I also need some company. Can we go somewhere and just talk… I'm not looking for a quick fuck… just someone… *real*… to talk to."

"*Real*, what do you mean?" I ask as she continues to hold my hand.

"I can see you are different. We were told, when I first started this… to look for the real folks… but so far, you are the only real person I've encountered… and I've been here since… well, for a while."

"Okay, you can come back to my hotel, I'll get you something to eat… and even a place to sleep… but I'm not into prostitutes… just so you know."

"That's fine… because I'm not a prostitute," she replies.

As she moves out of the shadows, and I see her up close… I am once again surprised at how good she looks. Her clothes are a bit shabby… shop-warm, and rather dirty, but her hair looks recently combed, and she does not smell bad. I try to detect her accent, and it is not of a 19th century London prostitute. "Okay, come along with me, we'll get you some clean clothes, something to eat… and something to drink."

"Thank you, kind sir… I will forever be in your debt." I want to reply that I am not interested in having someone in my debt, but decide to let it pass, as we walk down the streets of London, on our way back to my hotel.

Mutual Interests

We arrive at the hotel, I decide to be upfront, and we walk in through the main door. No one pays us any attention. We head up the three flights of stairs, down the hall, and I use my key to unlock the door.

Once inside, I light the kerosene lanterns, and offer the 'girl' a seat. "Sorry, I forgot to ask your name… I'm James," I state as I hold out my hand. The girl takes it, we shake and I check her fingernails. You can tell a lot about a person just by checking their fingernails… or at least I read that in a book somewhere.

"My name is Joyce Franklin, I'm from Detroit, Michigan. From your accent, I am guessing you are from the States, too."

"Yes, I am… I just arrived in London less than two weeks ago." I did not think Joyce sounded English. "What brings you to London? I assumed you were an original *Sim* since you stated you've been here for a while."

"It seems like forever, but actually, I've been here for about five years… James, I will be happy to answer and all of your questions, but May I please take a bath… you have actual hot water… and it's been so long."

"Sure, where are my manners? While you do that, there is a shop downstairs that sells lady fashions… what size are you, and I'll get you a couple of outfits."

"That is not really necessary… but I'm a size six."

I leave Joyce heading toward the bath. Yes, we have hot and cold running water… mostly cold… at least early in the morning. I am guessing Joyce is 20ish… so I pick out a couple of simple outfits… two dresses, a slip, couple pairs of underwear, and bras.

I have to guess at the bra size. The saleslady tries to talk me into buying the latest in feminine style… the girdle, but I pass.

I return and hear Joyce, singing in the tub… I smile, knock on the bathroom door, and announce, "Just dropping off these clothes," and make a point of slamming the door shut after I leave the clothes in a pile on the bath floor. I decide just to sit and wait it out. I am both hungry and… mostly in need of a drink. It's not that I'm feeling uncomfortable about taking in a perfect stranger, and I know that I will not take advantage of her situation… but her story line, accent… all of it… bothers me. I decide not to push too hard… first things first.

It is over an hour before Joyce exits the bath… but it was time well spent. The dress fits nicely… for a dress (try finding ladies slacks in 1890 London). "Ahhh… that is so much better. Thank you, James."

"Well, since I've bought you clothes, and you've used my bathtub… I guess we are on a first name basis… call me Jim."

"Thank you, Jim." Joyce walks over and holds out both hands, I hesitate. "Oh, don't worry, I will not throw myself on you… even though you deserve that, I just want to give you a hug."

I accept and we hug, but I pull away after just a few seconds. It's not that I'm a cold fish… but rather, I am already becoming quite attracted to Joyce… and do not want to tempt fate.

"You look great, now let's go out, have a few drinks, dinner… and you can tell me your story," I start.

"Great, I'll tell you mine, and you can tell me yours."

…

I break with tradition (two weeks of tradition, at least), and we head to what I have been told, by Fred, is the best restaurant in London. We don't have reservations, but I hand the *maître d'* my *Keycard* upon entry, and magically, we have a great table… overlooking the City of London.

"This is fantastic, Jim," Joyce states as we watch the gas lights of the city begin to come alive below us.

Our waiter arrives, "Drinks for the lady or the gentlemen?" he asks.

"Scotch for me... the best you have," I state.

"I'll have white wine, Chardonnay, if you have it," Joyce states.

I look at Joyce in disbelief, then at the waiter, "Give us a moment while we discuss things," I state, and the waiter leaves our table.

"What the heck, Joyce... Chardonnay... there is no such thing as Chardonnay in 1890 London... or in Detroit, for that matter. What are you? Where are you from?"

"Let's have a couple of drinks first, and I will tell you all about me... I believe you've earned that." The waiter returns with my scotch.

"Same for me, Joyce announces, but make mine a double."

I hold off on all questioning... the interrogation, until we are well into our second drink. We are both relaxed... I am finding Joyce quite interesting... almost fascinating, but now is the time to get some answers.... "So who are you, where are you from, and why are you here?" I begin, once we've finally ordered dinner.

"I am Joyce Franklin, I'm from Detroit, Michigan... just as I told you earlier."

"Maybe, but you are not from 1890... are you?" I ask, point blank.

I never said I was from 1890, now did I? You might have assumed that, but I never said it. So far, at least, I have not lied to you."

"Okay, when are you from... what is your *STR*?" I ask, just to see if she is paying attention.

"My space-time reference is... exactly the same as yours. I left the Earth, as we all knew it, on January 5th, 2054. I was told I would be participating in a great study... and important study... and that the study would last up to one year. Well, if this is the study, then the one year limit has long since passed. By the local time... I've been here at least five years... maybe even longer."

"And how old were you when you first arrived?"

"Twenty One… and if my mirror is at all accurate… I remain 21."

"And why were you hired… and who hired you?"

"As I said, I was hired to participate in a great study… a one year VR study… to see how long a human could live in a VR… Sim.…"

"And why would you take such an assignment?"

"Why do you think… we were offered big credit… very big credits."

"We… are there more of you?" I ask.

"Not as many as before… but I believe I may be the last of us remaining alive."

"What about the others… were they returned to… er… their place and time of origin?" I ask.

"No," Joyce replies, the rest of the 'girls' in the study have all been killed… by 'Jack the Ripper'.

Mystery Unfolds

Our dinner arrives at just that moment, so we begin to eat our food and defer the remaining conversation until... later. I would say how wonderful the food was... but honestly, I have very little memory of eating it. I did however order another double scotch, and so did Joyce.

We wait on the remainder of our discussion until we are back at the hotel. It is a fairly lengthy walk from the restaurant to the hotel, but we stay on the main streets, which are fairly well lit. We arrive, without incident, and walk up to our room.

"Could we finish this discussion tomorrow, Jim... I am rather... uh... how can I put this... drunk... yea that's the term I was looking for."

"Sure. I'll sleep on the coach, and you can have the bed... is there anything you need before we retire?" I ask.

"No, but you are welcomed to join me... if you care to," she replies.

"Not tonight. Let's complete our discussion in the morning, and then see where things lead to from there, okay?"

...

Not the most comfortable couch I've ever slept on, but then not near as bad as the swamp I spent the better part of a night in less than two weeks ago. Once I awake, I put the coffee on. 1890 London, as I am quickly finding out, is a rather primitive era. They drink tea over here, but Fred was able to find me some real coffee... and for that I am thankful. *Fred*... good, once Joyce and I complete our discussion... we will place a visit to ole Fred.

92

Over coffee and English pastries (courtesy of the local baker… delivered fresh every morning of the week), we pick up our discussion right were we left off. "So, are you telling me that the notorious 'Jack the Ripper' is killing real 'girls' and not Sims?"

"Yes, he has killed five of us so far… and I may be the last one remaining alive."

"Did you seek help from the police?" I ask.

"Police? Help? Are you kidding, they wanted to run me in for prostitution… told me if I wanted to be safe… then get off the street."

I had been hesitating to ask this… as it is rather personal and uncomfortable… but I believe now is the time. "So, are you 'girls' prostitutes?" I ask. Subtle, right?

"Not at first, no, but later, after the first year and we all found out we would not be going home, then we had to figure out a way to survive. So, yes, eventually, some of us became prostitutes, in order to survive."

"But, who were your clients… no humans are in the *Sim*?"

"Simply not true, Jim… there are humans in this *Sim*… and many of them are miserable, lonely, and need comfort… and some of us needed credits… to live, to survive."

"Okay, now I am not judging, but you appear to be educated… could you not find a real… job… somewhere in this big town?"

"An educated female in 1890 London… are you serious? Either you get married and have children, or you hit the streets. There is really, no choice."

"I assumed there were no humans in this *Sim*," I respond, just trying to understand the situation.

"And why is that? We were told there would be thousands to humans to interact with… and that was our job. To interact, assess if they were having a good time, what they liked… what they didn't like… and then feed that back to management."

"And you think that was maybe five years ago?"

"Yes, according to the local time we arrived in 1884… and now it's 1889. But, you still have not answered my question… why do you think there are no humans?"

"Well, you see it was like this…" and I begin a very short version of my own story… leaving out all of the times I've been killed, eaten, hung, stapled and mutilated. "So, the reason you see no humans is… the *Sim* actually never opened for business. With me, the owner/creator trapped in here these last ten years, I guess it just never seemed feasible to open it to the public."

We stop at this point. We both need a break, so I head out for the paper, and return from the lobby, with paper in hand, just a few minutes later.

"Something doesn't add up, here," Joyce announces, a few minutes after I begin reading the paper.

"Duh… really?" I respond, a bit sarcastically.

"No, what I mean is this… we were told the *LifeSim*™ game was open… had been open for at least a year… and that is how we were to be paid. For each survey we turned in, we got a hundred credit bonus… in addition to our thousand credit a day fee."

"So, you were told the game was open… and what year was this?"

"We left in 2054 and arrived in 1884."

"I got here in 2049 to do the final *Beta* before we officially opened… and since I never returned, I assumed the *Sim* game never opened. And… in the ten years I've been here… I have met only one… no maybe two other humans… the game is *definitely* not open," I conclude.

"I am not disputing that… only telling you what they told me and what I have personally experienced… there are humans here in the *Sim*."

"Understood," I reply… trying to think.

"So, why would they lie?" Joyce asks.

"Why, indeed?" I reply.

…

Since it looks as if Joyce may be here for a while, I decide that we should go shopping together… get everything she needs to make herself comfortable. Unfortunately, I cannot hand her my *Keycard*, 'here… go buy anything your cute little heart desires', since the *Keycard* is linked directly to my thumb print, and if someone else holds it in their hand for more than a few moments (long enough to insert it into the register and get the transaction approved), then it begins to glow a soft red, and the authorization circuits within the card are temporarily deactivated.

That happened to me once, several years back, the bartender forgot to return my *Keycard* after authorizing my service. It took ten minutes before it began to squeal (yes squeal... but not like a baby... more like a chalk board when fingernails are applied). The only way to stop that is for the authorized owner to hold the card, pressing firmly on the circle on the back, until the squealing stops, and the card turns first to green, and then to white (inactive state). Sorry, but I digress.

Our first stop is the front desk. "Lady Joyce will be joining me for a while, so two things. First, she needs her own key, and second, we need a larger room. Two bedrooms... and possibly two separate bath rooms."

"I can get you a larger suite, and one that has two bedrooms... although they are rather small... but we have no rooms that have more than a single bath. Most of the rooms, actually, share a common bath for the entire floor."

"Do what you can, please, cost is no object. Lady Joyce and I will be out shopping... please have our new accommodations ready by the time we return."

We head out shopping, but to my surprise, Joyce purchases very little, other than a few necessities, and basics (better quality soap, for one... yes the Lye soap is definitely a deal breaker). We stop for lunch at a small café we spot along the way, and are back at the hotel by 4PM.

Ronald, the resident and permanent front desk clerk, smiles as we entered the hotel, "We solved your problem, Mr. Caldwell and Lady Joyce... We vacated the entire top floor, and it is all yours. There are only three large suites up there, and nobody important was staying in them, at the moment, so we secured the entire floor for you... and of course any of your friends you might care to invite over."

"That is perfect, Ronald, thank you! Now since we are on the subject of service, is it possible to get room service...

someone to maybe bring us food, drinks, and provide other services... that sort of thing." I'm not certain what hotel services were available in 1889 London.

"Yes, based on the weekly fee for the entire top floor of the hotel, I am certain we can have a runner... or someone from the kitchen check on your needs every few hours... and provide those services."

Without further ado, we get our keys and head to our new Penthouse suite. Unfortunately, after securing the place where Kathy was/is staying... I am not too impressed, but, more importantly, Joyce is. "Oh, this is great, Jim, thank you. We walk through all three apartments, which are linked by a common door between each room. Joyce decides on the first room, I take the third, and we decide to use the center suite for our get-togethers, discussions... that sort of thing.

Since each apartment has its own entrance, I tell Joyce, "I won't come in through your room... but will head from the elevator directly down to my room. Here is your key, and anytime you want to bolt the door between us... do not even ask, just do it."

"That won't happen, Jim... my door is always open... but thanks!"

I head back down to the lobby (how did they live before *SmartComms*?), and make several service-related requests. I tell them, "Room 1002 will be our common quarters, and that is where the food and beverages should be served. Here is a list of what we want.... As soon as possible, please... but bring the scotch and ice first, please."

We spend our first night in our penthouse suite just talking, drinking, and eating. One of the runners comes up, makes us a nice fire, and so we sit close to it, and just enjoy life. That is one of the things I've learned to do in the ten years I've been here... try to enjoy myself. It took me a long time to learn that... but eventually, we must accept our fate, and get back into life, or *Sim*-life, as the case may be.

Nothing noteworthy comes out of our conversation this evening, and we decide to head to bed about midnight. "The offer to join me still stands," Joyce announces, but I smile, politely decline, and head to my own bedroom.

...

Breakfast is served as prearranged, at 8AM each morning in the 'common room'. Two morning papers are delivered, and the headlines are not good, "Ripper Strikes again!" Sometime last night, the sixth victim's body was discovered in a dark alley on the North side of London... actually only a few blocks from our hotel.

I read the article, twice, but decide to let Joyce lead any conversation related to 'Jack'. I am on my third cup of not-so-awful coffee, when Joyce drops the paper and states, "Let's talk, Jim."

"Sure, Joyce, you pick the topic..."

"You know the topic... JTR."

"Was she one of yours?" I ask.

"Her name was not disclosed and it is usually a week or more before the 'official coroner's report' is available and I can check the list... but I am assuming so. I thought I was the last... but it is possible that other females came through after our first group arrived. We must do something about this situation."

"What do you have in mind, Joyce?" I ask.

"I have nothing in mind... brains are your department... not mine!"

"Well, now, let's not sell ourselves short, or create any undo expectations, Joyce... let's discuss the situation, and if we come up with any... usable... ideas, then we can form a plan." I hate to be non-committal, but I have no idea how to stop Jack the Ripper from killing innocent young women.

It is already noon, and neither of us has come up with a single idea. I break out the Scotch... the creative juice of life (No, Joyce didn't laugh either). "Okay, let's try and relax and think outside the box," I state as I close my eyes and sip my scotch. An idea immediately comes to mind, "I do not have a clue how to stop Jack... but let's see if we can find any other potential candidates and bring them here… to safety," I state. "We certainly have plenty of room…"

"Jim, you are wonderful, and I did think of that…but… I've no idea of the whereabouts of any of the…the other 'girls'. We parted ways several years back…decided to 'divide and conquer' and I very seldom see any of them… and with the new arrivals…I would not begin to know where to look for any other the remaining girls," Joyce declares.

Witch Hunt…

"So, when was the last time you saw any of the other 'girls' and where?" I ask.

"Oh, hell, Jim… this is not going to work. We could spend months looking in every dark alley in this damn town… and never find them. 'Night girls' are only found when they want to be found."

"Okay, so we agree not to walk through downtown London, hand in hand, hollering, 'Betty Joe… Clair Marcie… where the hell are you? I guess we are back to square one."

We are, once again, reading the morning paper. I am about finished, so check the personals, they are always good for a laugh or two, "Ahh… two kittens are missing, and the owner is offering a Penny reward," I state, just to pass the time. "She must really love those kittens." That reminds me of something… it's in the back of my mind… and now on the tip of my tongue… but wait, I must have swallowed it.

Joyce looks up from the paper, eyes twinkling, "Yes, Jim… that's it."

"What's it?"

"Let's run an ad in the personals… looking for the girls…"

Something like, "Prostitutes wanted… call my cell 24/7?" I state.

"Morbid. No, but we do have a secret code-word… actually a few of them. We called ourselves The Bobbsey Twins.

"I don't get that reference?" I state.

"An old early to mid-1900's book series about these… rich kids… doesn't really mean anything… but it would uniquely identify us… without a doubt. Let me take a stab at creating it… where is that quill pen when I need it," Joyce states.

"But would the new arrives understand the reference?"

"Hopefully... there were dozens of us back in training... and we made that reference before any of us came through to Sim-ville?

An hour later, we have our personal add.

Sister Joyce searching for her Bobbsey Twins

I am safe now and want the same for my remaining family. Please leave a message at the Fairmont Hotel, box 221. I love you all!

"Perfect... and when will this ad run?" I ask.

"I have no idea of the lead time... but let's head down to *The Illustrated London News* office... and find out."

On our way out, we stop by the desk, "I would like to rent a post box... and also need to know immediately, if I receive any mail."

Sure, Mr. Caldwell. We have all of these to choose from... Would you like box 1?"

"No, how about 221?'

"You got it. No additional charge... thank you for your continued patronage."

"Okay, but remember, if anyone drops a letter or post in this box, Joyce or I need to be notified immediately."

"Do you want me to retain him or her?"

"Retain... is that even legal?"

"There is no law that I know of preventing me from retaining someone on suspicion..."

"Suspicion of what?"

"Suspicion of... anything."

"No, but can you have someone follow them... if they decide to leave the hotel and not wait for an answer?"

"I must say, Mr. Caldwell... you are a weird guy... no offense intended."

"None taken... if you can hold them... by offering them free food... or a drink... that would be good... but not forcibly."

"Okay, sir, we will do our best... under these... constricting circumstances."

Joyce and I head over to the *London News* office, and we place our ad. The newspaper containing the ad will come out in four days. I hand them my *Keycard*... they look at me funny, but then Joyce hands them a note. They smile, take the note, and return the change.

On our way out of the newspaper office, Joyce explains, "While most of the main establishments like restaurants, hotels, and bars accept your *Keycard*... some of the outlier businesses do not. I am not sure why... but it's a fact. Sometimes, Notes talk and *Keycards* walks. Another thing I would look into... if I had the time or the inclination... of which... I have neither.

...

I continue my daily trek through London... looking for the escape hatch. Nothing. I would be discouraged, but passed that historical landmark about six years ago. I continue looking for the exit door because I have no choice... but one day... there will be a clue... and when I find it... new doors will begin to open.

I have a secondary mission, as of late, and that is looking for prostitutes. No, not for my personal consumption but just to see if any of them are a member of the Bobbsey Twins.

I am on my way back to the hotel... another wasted day... I am tired, I am bored... but I am looking forward to seeing Joyce. As I pass an alleyway, I look in, as I always do, and spot a female. I stop, turn and head into the alley, "Care for quickie, mister... only a quid... come this way."

Her Cockney accent gives her away, but I ask anyway... "Are you one of the Bobbsey Twins?"

"I can be anything you want, Governor... for two quid's... I can be the queen of England". I hand her a pound note, turn and leave...

...

I stop by the front desk, but then remember it will be two more days before the Personal ad makes the paper. Ronald is there, as usually, and asks, "How is your day going, Mr. Caldwell?"

"Good, and you?"

"So, so."

As I approach the Penthouse elevator, I reflect on that... not a valid response... not at all. I arrive at the elevator. Ring the bell, and in moments the elevator arrives, "Yes, sir, Mr. Caldwell... step right in."

He closes the gate and we ascend the ten floors to the Penthouse. Buddy opens the gate, and states, "Your floor, sir... have a good evening."

I head down the hallway to my room, and enter. Joyce is sitting in a high back Queen Anne chair, sipping a scotch, "Join me?" she asks. I nod, head over to the kitchenette, and pour myself a scotch. I reach into the ice box, retrieve a couple of cubes, and head back over to Joyce. "And how was your day?" I ask as I take a seat in the Queen Anne across from Joyce.

"Lonely. Boring... but also... wonderful. Have I told you lately how much I appreciate what you've done for me?"

"Yes, you have and you are welcome." I detect a bit of a slur in Joyce's speech, but decide not to judge, and take my first sip.

"What were you up to today, Jim?" Joyce asks.

"Oh, the usual boring shit... looking for exit doors that do not exist... attempting to find Bobbsey twins... that do not exist."

"There're out there, but if you go looking for them in dark alleys... you will never find them." I am quickly becoming uncomfortable with the looks I am receiving from Joyce. "Let's go to dinner... I'm hungry."

"So am I, but, not for dinner."

I fall into the trap, "For what when?"

"For you... it's been long enough... quit fighting it... let it happen... Make love to me!"

I look at Joyce, directly into her eyes... I refuse to take advantage of someone... because they are drunk, or think they owe me a debt of gratitude. "No, Joyce, not like this... let me get some coffee going..."

"Fuck coffee, Jim, I want you. If you are not attracted to me, then just say so…"

"Oh, no, it's not that."

"Then what is it?"

"I do not want to take advantage of the situation… of you."

"Okay, fair, enough. But, what if I want to take advantage of you?"

…

Never being one to compare sex between different women… I still have to say, "Wow that was the best sex ever." We make love for hours, in several ways… but finally, we are satisfied. She holds me, we cuddle, and soon fall asleep.

Regrets

I awake and am alone in bed. I immediately regret having sex with Joyce. Oh, it is not that I didn't enjoy it... it was fantastic... but it means, that one day soon... I will be leaving this place... and Joyce will not be coming with me. And, at this very moment, I find that eventuality totally unacceptable.

I make my way to the common area, and Joyce is setting there looking gorgeous, sipping coffee.

"Good morning... coffee on the stove," she states.

I get my cup, and sit down beside her. She takes my hand. "Best night ever!" she states.

I'm hooked... and in Love! "What are we going to do?" I ask.

"About what? The ad comes out tomorrow, so hopefully..."

"No, I mean, about us. I have explained the situation, and I know you understand that soon... I will be *Reset* and be gone... probably forever."

"Yes, but is that a sufficient reason not to make love to me... I think not. Do you regret it?'

"Absolutely not... but now, I can't leave you... it will break my heart."

"We all have to do shit we don't like... such is the way of life. But, I could not allow the sexual tension between us to continue without bringing it to a climax, so to speak," Joyce smiles.

"Well, it was a good climax... I must admit... but what now?" I ask.

"We wait for the ad to come out... and hopefully, at least some of my sisters will show up... before it's too late."

...

We spend the day, and night, mostly in bed, having sex, and Joyce is wonderful. I awake and check my *SmartComm*. It is 6PM, and we need to get out of here... eat... and be ready for tomorrow.

"We are sitting in *McGillacutty's* having dinner, when Joyce decides to talk, "I have not told you this before, but back in 2054... when I took this assignment... I was running away from something."

"We are all running away from something, Joyce... I've been running most of my life..."

"Yea, but I need to tell you about... now that I know I love you... I must be honest."

"Oh, God... please don't tell me about all the guys you've fucked, drugs you taken, or hearts you've broken. It simply is not necessary. We all have a past, Joyce... but that is the key word... PAST... let's leave it there, and find a way to live... survive in the present... because soon, the future will arrive... and things will change."

...

Joyce nods, and discontinues the discussion. Even if she's killed someone... back there in 2054... I don't care... I love her and want every minute we have left to account for something. We leave the restaurant early, it is still light out, so we decide to take a tour of London... the London of our dreams... and not the real 1890's London. We see Big Ben. It was created back in 1859, I believe, but might need to check that fact. We walk around, looking at the Thames River, enjoying the evening. But soon, it is nightfall, and so we head back to the hotel. "Let's stop for a final drink, if that is okay?" I offer.

"As long as we are together... I do not care what we do," Joyce replies as we continue holding hands and walking back toward our hotel.

We pass Fred's, and I decide that maybe it's the time to have that talk with Fred. We walk in, but the feel is different, and Fred is not at the bar. "What can I get you two... a couple of pints of the house specialty?" The barkeep offers.

"No, where is Fred?" I ask.

"I have no idea who Fred is. The GM is a guy named Wesley, but he never works the evening shift... only the lunch crowd... what can I get you?" the bar-keep asks, for the second time.

I do not reply, but continue holding Joyce's hand, turn and head back into the street. Once outside, I look up at the sign, it looks similar to the old sign but reads, *ENG Pub 'n Grill*. I look at Joyce, "Let's go home."

...

The next morning, there is a knock. It is breakfast and the local paper... today is the day. Joyce grabs the paper, leafs through to the personals and locates her ad. "Looks great, Jim. Bold type... good position... now we'll just have to wait to see if we get any hits."

While I am happy about the ad, and hopeful we can soon secure some or all of Joyce's Bobbsey Twins, I am a bit down regarding Fred. Being the creator of the *LifeSim™ Game*, I thought I understood the rules of that game. And rule number one is continuity... bars do not go out of business in a *Sim*, to be replaced by other bars... that is actually... absurd.

I decide not to disclose any of this interesting but quite irrelevant information to Joyce... at least until we can deal with her immediate issues... I'll table these other personal issues... until later.

Nothing happens this day, but we are in the hotel room the next morning, just recovering from our daily extreme sex workout, when there is a knock on the door. "Mr. Caldwell, a lady... in the lobby... left a note... please hurry."

We go from nude to clothed in less than a minute, and we are out the door. The elevator is waiting, we enter, and make the painfully slow descent to the lobby. The gate finally opens, and we run to the front desk. Ronald is there, "She just left... I believe she turned left after leaving the hotel."

We quickly run out of the hotel, turn left and begin running down one of the main streets of London. I follow Joyce, since I have no idea what any of the 'girls' actual look like.

We continue a block, but find nothing. Joyce stops, looks at me, "Lost her, damn."

"Let's not give up... let's go back and check the message... maybe she has given us some information we can use."

We slowly walk back to the hotel, and up to the desk. Ronald hands us the note, "Sorry I could not detain her, but the moment she handed me the note and said 'Box 221", she turned and walked right out. "I sent the lad up to tell you, but well..."

Joyce takes the note, and we head over to the lounge area to read it. We both take seats on the large and ornate sofa. I wait.

After a few moments, "Okay, it is from Brenda, I remember her back in orientation. She is scared and thinks this might be a trap... so she sent me some cryptic information. If we are able to decode it, then we should be able to locate her."

"Did she say anything about the others?" I ask.

"Nothing. Her note basically describes some of the earlier scenarios we were involved in, during our orientation. Only myself and the other 'girls' would understand any of this... so let's head back upstairs, and let me try to decode the message and maybe get us a meeting time and location."

I have a thought, "Let's go back to that bar down the street... and while you are trying to figure out the message... I'll be having a conversation with the GM... I am beginning to accumulate a lot of unanswered questions... and I need to start getting at least some answers."

Joyce is up for a drink or two, so we walk down the block to *ENG Pub 'n Grill*, as it has been renamed. We take a seat at one of the many empty tables... away from the bar. I head up to the bar, "Are you the new GM?" I ask to the fortyish looking English gentleman behind the counter,

"I am indeed the GM... but not new... been here ten years this summer. What can I get you laddie?" He asks in the thickest English accent I've encountered since I've been here.

"Sorry, to dispute you, sir," I begin, "but I've been coming here for several week now... and up to two days ago this was *Fred's Place*," I state as I look the Sim in the eyes.

"And who might you be... to be asking these questions?" he responds, but does not stop polishing the glasses. I turn back toward Joyce, and see a young lassie taking her order, so return my attention to the GM.

"I am James Caldwell, the creator of this world, and who, sir, are you?" I ask but do not offer my hand in friendship.

"I am the General Manager... Mike Belkin, but my friends call me Mickey."

"You have not answered my original question... where is Fred and why was this bar... modified."

"I have no idea what you are talking about. As I've said, in case you were not listening, I have been the GM here at the pub for ten years."

"You sir, are a liar!" I decide to raise my voice, and call his bluff.

Two other guys... mid-twenties are seated at the bar, "You need any help, Mr. Belkin," they ask.

"Thanks laddies... but this is just a misunderstanding... enjoy your drinks... then get along home with you both." As if on cue, both boys finish their pints and leave the pub.

We are alone, but, as of yet, Mickey has not stopped polishing those damn glasses. "Mickey, while I realize you are just a *Sim*, I also understand the underlining directives and programming that all Sims undergo before they are activated, and allowed to work in any establishment that services the public. While you do not have to give out information not specifically relevant to your job, you cannot actually lie to a customer either. So let's test that out shall we? First, are you a *Sim* created by the *FgU llc?*"

"Yes, I am."

"What is your serial number?"

"Series C.JC182731."

"How long have you been the GM of this Pub?"

"Nine years, eight months, and seventeen days."

Well, I did not see that coming. "What happened to *Fred's Place*?"

"Never heard of it."

I have one last card up my sleeve... and decide now is the time to play it. I retrieve my *Keycard*, and throw it on the counter. "Pick up the card, please, sir."

Mickey looks down at the counter, picks up my *Keycard*, studies it, turns it over a few times and returns it to the counter. "What exactly am I looking at here? What is this material? It's not glass or wood... I have no idea what this means."

No wink of the eye... no change in facial expressions... it's as if... "Okay, never mind Mickey... I'm just here with my friend to have a good time... sorry to have bothered you," I state, hoping he will not have us tossed out of the Pub. Been there, done that, and have the bruised butt to prove it.

I turn and head back to the table. The scotches have arrived, and Joyce is still heads-down reading the message, scribbling something on an old sheet of paper. I briefly glance back at Mickey, but he has returned to polishing his glasses... what the fuck is this all about?

I sip my scotch and wait on Joyce. She finally looks up, "What was that about?" she asks.

"You don't want to know... any luck translating, rather, decoding the message?" I ask.

"Yes, I believe I've got it. There is the warehouse where we originally arrived, and we often met there, even after we all decided to head in different directions. There is an old saying back in 2050... which I'm sure you remember, '*Before the moon is full... the world is cruel.*'"

"Yes, I remember that... but what does that have to do with this situation?" I ask.

"One of our 'sisters' Sally... used to say that, every day at exactly 5PM. It was something she and her old boyfriend used as code that said... time to head home and Fu... have sex. We all thought it was funny, and it became a common expression to denote... time for a drink... time for... well virtually anything. So, we are to meet Brenda at the warehouse at 5PM today."

I check my *SmartComm*... it is after 3PM. We decide to finish our scotches, and then head to the warehouse, which Joyce assures me, is less than 20 minutes away. Our lassie's (cocktail waitress) name is Glenda, and she is super friendly, almost to a fault. She asks a ton of questions, where are we from, how long have we been in town... when are we leaving...? The total third degree. We order our final drink, and Glenda heads off to get our drinks, "Damn that Glenda is rather aggressive," I offer.

"Funny you say that, because at first, before you came to the table, she said very little. She brought my drink and left. Yes, you are right... since you got here she has been all over us. Jim, what the hell is going on?"

"We'll talk about that later... let's finish our drink and then head to the warehouse... we will not be coming back here."

Obviously, I will not be able to pay the tab with my *Keycard*, but, I always have the local currency, in my pocket... for such occasions. I leave two one pound notes... way too much, and we head toward the warehouse.

We arrive outside the warehouse at 4:55PM. "Are we going in?" I ask.

"No, that was part of the code... we originally arrived behind the warehouse... there is a park... but let's wait until exactly five." Joyce continues to walk around the warehouse... and I follow along, like a puppy dog.

At exactly 5Pm, Joyce takes my hand and we walk down the alley next to the warehouse, turn left, and there is a small park, some children are playing... and that gives us both a high level of comfort. We sit at the first park bench we find... and wait. At 5:09PM, a young girl slowly walks toward us, passes us by, but then returns, "Is this seat taken?" she asks.

Joyce slips over, and 'Brenda' takes a seat next to her... on the far end of the bench. They talk quietly for a while. Neither of them look directly at me, but engage in their own personal conversation. They mostly whisper... but occasionally one or the other raises their voice, and I am able to pick up a bit of their conversation.

It is almost 5:30PM before Joyce, glances over at me. "Brenda will follow us back to the hotel. She is terribly freighted… but we'll discuss that later. Let's get her back home safely… and then go from there."

Joyce and I get up from the bench, Joyce talks my hand and we 'stroll' back in the direction of the hotel. I do not glance back, just in case someone is watching us… and once we are inside the hotel, we head to the elevator, and make the slow assent to our room.

Rescue Mission

We do not speak until we are actually inside the hotel suite. Joyce leads the way, and we head into the middle suite, where she offers Brenda a seat and then introduces me. "This is our lord and savior, Sir James Caldwell. You may not believe this, but Jim actually invented the game... but before you go beating on him... he is stuck here just like the rest of us. He is trying to find a way out... but until that happens, at least he is offering us a better life."

"Brenda, what would you like to drink?" I offer as my first formal communication with her.

"Anything with alcohol will work," she replies. I get up and return with three scotches. I put them on the table, Brenda picks up her glass... and drinks the entire thing... without stopping... big mistake.

I return to the kitchen and get a glass of water, and she drinks that down. "Damn that was good," Brenda states after her coughing fit stops... or at least slows down.

"Another... please?" she offers.

I return with another scotch... and this time she takes only a small sip. "I know this is just a dream and I will awake soon... but please... let me enjoy it as long as I can... do not make me go back out on those streets tonight..."

"You may never have to go back to the streets, Brenda... If I can prevent that."

"You are the lord and savior," Brenda replies.

"No, but as Joyce indicated, I am the inventor of this game... although that fact does not seem to be pulling as much weight as it used to," I state.

"What does that mean?" Joyce asks.

"We'll talk later… but for now… I'll bet the first thing Brenda would like is a bath… Joyce, would you do the honors. I will order us some food… be back in a few minutes."

"How about clothes?" Joyce asks. "What size are you, Brenda?" I ask.

"Same as Joyce… don't you remember… all of us 'girls' are exactly the same size… a six."

…

While the girls bathe (I don't want to even think about it), I head down to the lobby, and walk into the kitchen. I order double food for the night, to be delivered ASAP, and then head out to the nearest dress shop. I collect similar, but not the same articles for Brenda as I previously purchased for Joyce. I assume they can share clothes… but Joyce and I have not discussed this… detail.

Remembering some of the other personal requirements, I next head over to the sundry shop and pick up some of the other necessities of life… like real soap… and get a few trinkets that I see, and think Brenda might like.

I am back at the hotel in less than an hour. I head to my suite and wait for Joyce to give me the 'all clear' sign. I leave Brenda's clothes just inside the door… and wait. She knocks on the connecting door (we decided to keep it closed until Brenda becomes 'comfortable' with our open relationship).

I open the door and Joyce is smiling, "May I introduce the real Brenda Palmer."

Brenda walks out… I am impressed, "Have we met… I'm certain I would have remembered," I offer. There is a startling transition. Now, to be honest, Brenda is nowhere near a beautiful as Joyce… but she is, nonetheless, a stunning and attractive female.

Brenda and I hug, "No we've never met before… you have a face I would never forget."

Before we get too comfortable in our mutual admiration society, there is a knock on the door. Brenda is immediately frightened, but Joyce explains, "It's just the laddie with our food

113

order... no one gets up on this floor without authorization... so stop worrying, relax and enjoy."

The laddie wheels in a huge food cart, plus there is Champaign... it will be a celebration... to life, to love... and to the hope for a future rescue.

...

It is a pleasant and relaxing, if not entertaining, evening. We go slow, trying not to overwhelm Brenda... but make her feel welcomed... and safe. We finally head for bed slightly after midnight.

Joyce is in charge of that activity, "This is your bedroom, Brenda... but, I just need to warn you... if you make any attempt to end up in bed with Jim... you will be out in the street, and on your ass before dawn."

Joyce returns smiling, "Brenda is happy... and their may be others."

No one else answers Joyce's personal ad, so we decide to print a second ad... this one even larger than the first.

...

However, after a week has passed, and the second newspaper ad comes out... we have not gotten any further hits... no messages. Joyce and I have been taking it easy on Brenda, allowing her time to mend... heal... and just recuperate from her recent ordeal. But, we decide, it is time to talk to Brenda, and form a new game plan to save the remaining girls... this plan seems to have run its course.

Over cocktails in the Parlor (as we've formally named the common living area in the center suite), Joyce opens the discussion, "Well, it doesn't look as if we are going to get any more hits based on our newspaper ad. Brenda, do you have any suggestions... ways that maybe we can get into contact with the other girls?"

"I've been thinking about that ever since I arrived here with you guys. If the girls aren't reading the paper... which is a high probably... I found your ad in a paper left at a park bench; then I have no clues. If they are like me, they are scared shitless. Probably hiding in alleyways... staying out of sight... like I did."

"Yea, me too Brenda, but when I say Jim walk by, I just knew he was real... and so I approached him. It was a risk, but paid off big time. Not sure how the others are reacting to the situations, especially since 'Jack' entered the picture."

"Yea, life was not great before that happened... but ever since, it's been living hell."

Okay, my turn to interject... and make everyone uncomfortable, "I need to bring this up, and sorry if this makes you uneasy, by why is 'Jack' targeting just you girls... you specific girls?"

"I have no idea... and are you sure that's what's happening... I was unaware of that..." Brenda replies, and she does now seem a bit more agitated.

Joyce takes hold of her hand, "I figured that out, Brenda... so far all of the girls who've been killed, have been our team members, no one else."

"That does not make sense," Brenda replies, "How could a *Sim* kill a real human... is that possible?"

"Absolutely," I reply. "I've been killed hundreds of times in the last ten years. The game allows for that."

"But," Brenda reminds me, "They are reset back into the game... right?"

"Yea, that is right... hum... I'm now wondering if the 'girls' who have been murdered... refused *Reset*, and went back to their lives... I had not thought about that," I add.

"So, if that is the case... and you've been killed a hundred times, as you claim, then why are you here?"

"Good question... I'm not sure. The first few times I was killed, I was still in *Beta* test mode, and assumed I was in auto-random-reset mode, but after a few months... I simply stopped thinking about it and concentrated more on living... death is painful... and I would not recommend it as a way out of here."

"But, at least that gives us some hope, Jim," Joyce responds, "If we do get out of the game after we die… then that is better than living in this damn Sim for the rest of… eternity."

"Yes, but since we are not sure that is what happens… I would recommend you stay away from 'Jack'," I reply.

"Agreed!" both girls respond.

Dealing with Reality

"I hate to bring this up but while we are on the subject of death, I need to remind you both... that soon... I will be *Reset* and will not be returning to this *STR*." I look at them both, and can see from their facial expressions, they are firmly in denial.

"I understand you do not want to discuss this, but it is not something that *might* happen... one day in the next five or ten years, it is something that *will* happen, anytime with the next few weeks."

"Since we can't do anything about that, Jim, then why bring it up at all? Once you leave... the hole will be so large... that maybe I'll just decide to crawl through it and met you on the other side."

"What does that mean, Joyce?" I ask.

"You know exactly what it means... *suicide* is always an option... and I had much rather die by my own hands then allow 'Jack' to decide my fate."

"But, there is no guarantee you will be *Reset* back into reality... you might really... just die!" I offer. "Or, even worse, you may *Reset* into another *STR* within the *Game*, like me. Remember, *the devil you know is better than the one you don't.*"

"Maybe... but it is an option," Joyce replies, as she heads to the kitchen for a refill. Brenda and I follow. So, once again, nothing is resolved, and no further plans are made. We are at a standstill... but at least two of the 'girls' are safe... and if I leave London, unexpectedly... they are much better off than when I arrived.

...

117

Joyce and I are up for heading to a nice restaurant for dinner, but Brenda has yet to overcome her fear, "You too go ahead, and I'll just eat from the food trey they serve at five," Brenda announces.

"No," I reply, "we can all stay here... until you are ready to venture out."

"But, Jim, as you said, you could be reset at any moment... so I would suggest that you and Joyce make the best of your time together... I can take care of myself."

I leave the decision up to Joyce, and she agrees with Brenda, "At least we know you are safe here in the suite... anywhere in the hotel for that matter."

"Are you two sure? I really don't mind eating in tonight?" I question.

"Nope," Brenda offers... "You guys go out... relax and enjoy. Have I told you how much I appreciate all that you've done for me?"

"Not in the last ten minutes," Joyce replies as she takes Brenda's hand, "We won't be too late. London basically closes at midnight... see you tomorrow."

"Be sure to stick to the well-lit areas, and keep away from the zombies," Brenda offers, with a smile.

...

Joyce and I decide to go back to *McGillacutty's* for dinner, and we do enjoy ourselves. Tonight is Shakespeare play night... and this time it's *Macbeth*. We drink, eat, and watch all three acts. It is an excellent performance, the best either of us has seen. As I've stated before, and will not dwell on... English food is not my favorite, but it is beginning to grow on me. The Mutton stew was quite delicious. We walk back from the restaurant/playhouse, hand in hand. It is a wonderful tonight. No fog, it is not raining, and the temp is maybe sixty degrees. A full moon is out... and, at least for now, 1890s London is a good place to be.

I stop by the front desk to say goodnight to Ronald, but he is not at his station. That has never happened below, I scan around and I see none of the usual *Sims*. I take Joyce's hand and we head quickly to the elevator. The elevator is here... the gate is open, but the operator is nowhere in sight. I take control, and push the lever up... and we ascend to the penthouse. We both rush down to the Parlor, let ourselves in... and Joyce yells, "Brenda where are you... we're home."

Joyce lets go my hand, and runs to Brenda's bedroom. I am right behind, but before I arrive, I hear the scream. I run in and look around... blood and body parts are everywhere. On the floor, the walls, even the ceiling. The last thing I see before I begin to tingle... getting ready to *Reset,* is Joyce, stooped over Brenda's mangled and mutilated torso, crying as she is begins throwing up her dinner.

Part 2

I May Have to Live It… But I Don't Have to Like It

Denial

I awake and it takes a few minutes for my mind to clear, and my memories to begin to return. At first, I remember... I am in the *Game*... the *Sim*. I've been here for... eleven years I believe. I see the castle up ahead... and begin to remember more. There will be monsters... maybe lots of them. And in order to get into the *Game*... which is usually in the *City*, I have to escape those monsters... otherwise I will be *Reset* and be required to try again... and again.

As I walk toward the castle, other memories begin to come into my head. I remember Kathy... and hope she is doing well. I remember my trip to Egypt, to see the Pyramids... that was a great trip right up until I became surrounded by those mummies... and then literally suffocated to death.

Then my other deaths begin coming back... I am freighted... stop and move away from the castle. How many times have I died? A dozen... no a hundred... I no longer keep count.

Survival is a powerful instinct, and from what I am now remembering, I must get through the castle and find my way to the *City*... in order to survive to play the *Game*... hoping to find a way out of here.

The question comes into my mind... why would I even want to survive... after all that has happened? I spot a large oak tree up ahead, head over to it, sit down, with my back against the giant oak, and look out over the castle.

For some reason, I am very tired. I don't remember being tired after a *Reset*... usually I'm refreshed, and ready to 'get back into the game'.

So what is different? Part of my mind wants to figure that out, but most of it refuses to deal with the pain, suffering, and sorrow. But I've been through pain hundreds of times... and ... but now I remember Joyce. Oh, My God... where is Joyce? I stand and look around... she was here just a moment ago... we had just gone to dinner and a play... Shakespeare... Macbeth. We were heading back to the hotel...

I stop, my feet become unstable. I fall to the ground... OH MY GOD... THE BASTARD KILLED BRENDA!

I sob... I can't stop crying... I don't want to ever stop crying... the love of my life is gone... forever... and our friend Brenda... I see the body parts strewn all over the floor... blood everywhere... my mind cannot handle it... so it decides to leave... for a while.

...

I awake and I am looking at the castle. It is, maybe a mile away. It is still daylight but dusk is fast approaching, and I understand I cannot be in the woods after dark. I start to get to my feet, but then think about Joyce... and Brenda... and fall back to the ground. "Fuck It!" I shout... "Let them eat me... and I hope they throw up from all of the excess fat!"

The sun retreats below the horizon, and the last thing I remember is the full moon rising, and thinking, it is gorgeous. I never see them, but they are suddenly upon me... the sound of my flesh ripping apart is horrifying... but fortunately, one of them quickly hits my jugular vein... and I...

All Our Yesterdays

I awake and I am royally pissed. I remember everything… and I decide I am not going to take it anymore. I spot the castle… and I begin to run toward it. As I get closer I start to shout, "Bastards… Monsters… I am coming for you…"

I am inside the castle and see the stairway ahead… fuck the stairway… I head left into an area I've never entered before… into pitch darkness. But not for long… at first, four red eyes appear… then eight, then sixteen. "Bring it on," I shout as I head into the mass of monsters who are waiting for me… hungry for my flesh. "Take this you bastards," I shout, as I begin tearing into them… tearing off their limbs… heads… but finally, in the end… the result is the same, but this time my last painful thought is… "So I die… I could give a shit!"

...

As happens on occasion, sometimes there is no castle. And for that I am not grateful. I am quite content spending the remainder of eternity fighting the monsters. This time, I decide, if I meet any monsters… then I will eat them… mutilate them… let them see how it feels to be the victim, for a change.

I approach the ridge, and there is the *City*. Maybe 23rd century… not sure… The city is floating above the ground… one of my personal fav effects. But for some reason, I really don't give a rat's ass about this city. Not sure what I give a damn about… if anything.

I check my *SmartComm* for the *STR*… 'Still calculating', it replies. My *SmartComm* remains in my hand. I look down at it… "What the fuck good are you," I state as I prepare to throw it as far away from me as possible... but I stop... and remember. All of the timelines I've ever visited are stored in that *SmartComm.* What good that will do me? I have no idea... but it is my only link to the past... and my continued sanity may require me to be linked to the past.

I reluctantly head toward the city. What choice do I have? I can't seem to die! Well actually that is not true, let me restate... I cannot seem to stay dead.

As I approach the *SkyCity*, despite my best efforts, and I am increasingly anticipating my arrival... what will life be like in the 23rd century? A *Sky City*... but then I remember my recent past... Joyce... Brenda! I understand that I should not hang on to my despair or anger... and the past... but damn them all... I love Joyce and want her back... and poor Brenda... what did she do to deserve such a horrible death! *"Fuck the person who created this horror show... fuck me!"* I shout to apparently no one.

I finally arrive below the city, and search for a way in, or up, as the case may be. I assume there will be some sort of elevator, or teleport mechanism, but as I scan the immediate area... I see nothing. I begin walking the path I spot ahead. It is a combination forest, recreational area, has a river flowing through it... very nice. I begin to relax and start to enjoy, but then remember... go back and rediscover my anger... I will never let it go...NEVER!!

...

I have been below the *SkyCity* for almost a week, and have not discovered a way in. That certainly does not make any sense... not that I really give a shit.

...

It has now been ten days, and I am thinking about why I cannot locate the entrance to the *SkyCity*. I have walked everywhere... maybe twenty miles... no entrance way... no access port... how the hell am I supposed to get up there?"

...

Finally, after two weeks, I encounter my first beings. It is a young couple, holding hands and strolling along the path between the park and the river. As I approach them, I ask, "Can you help me please... How do I get up to the *SkyCity*...? I've been looking for the entrance way for a couple of weeks now."

The male looks at the female, and then replies, "Why, there are entry portals everywhere... you must have passed a dozen in the last mile."

"What do they look like?" I ask.

The female answers, "They look like entry ways to the City... what else would they look like?"

I look at them both, but they just stare at me, then the female reaches over, whispers something to the male, and he turns to me as they begin to walk away. "Purity of thought... that is the key that unlocks all doors in *CloudCity*... have a wonderful day." With that said, the couple returns to holding hands, and continues down the path and out of sight.

"What does that mean?" I ask myself, "Purity of thought?"

I continue walking the path for another mile, looking for the entrance way, but find nothing. I begin to think about what the couple said, "Purity of thought", that must be a password of some sort... but a password to what?

I have no clue. I spot a park bench up ahead, and decide to sit, think, contemplate... and reflect upon the worse month of my entire life.

I sit, but I have trouble relaxing. How long has it been since I've relaxed... well, actually, I can answer that question to the very moment. The moment I saw the pieces of Brenda's body, scattered across the floor, on the bed, and pieces flung against the wall... well, that was the end of relaxing... maybe forever. It was also the end of peace, harmony, love and any other positive aspect of my sorry ass life. If I ever had any 'purity', it is certainly long gone...

127

"Purity of thought"… if only. I don't see how that is even remotely possible… not after what I've been through. My mind refuses to accept this as the answer, which is just as well, since that virtue has, recently, become quite an impossibility for me to obtain.

I decide just to sit on the bench… and I remain there for the remainder of the day, and into the night. I am not worried about monsters, zombies, vampires… or even Jack the ripper getting me at this point… since I no longer care if I live or if I die.

I awake the next morning to birds singling. It is such a pleasant sound, that without thinking about my recent past, I begin to smile. I am fully awake, and decide to head back toward the river… since I seem to have reached the far edge of the *SkyCity* above. Fortunately, there are lots of berries, and eatable fruit on bushes and trees throughout the area, and I partake of them as needed.

Finally, I arrive at the river. It is maybe a half-mile wide, and flowing rather briskly. I hear some loud noises coming from up stream. I look up and several young kids are playing at the edge of the water. I search, and spot their parents, sitting on the bank, right above them.

Having nothing better to do at the moment, I decide to watch the children as they play at the water's edge. At first, their games are mild and appear to be good clean fun. There are two boys and three girls, ranging in age from maybe ten to fourteen. But, apparently there is a disagreement, and one of the boys begins to shout at the other. The second boy is at the edge of river, just a few feet away from the current, He is paddling along, apparently ignoring the boy on shore who is shouting. As I watch, I see the boy on the bank, shout something else, but the boy in the water is apparently not listening. The boy on the bank searches around the bank, finds what looks like a medium sized rock, picks it up, and yells something else at the boy in the water.

The second boy further ignores him, and it is obvious, the boy of the bank is becoming quite agitated. I look over at the parents, and see the male, begin to stand up and say something to the boy on the bank. I look back at the boy on the bank, he has the rock in his hand, he stares down at it, and then looks at the boy at the water's edge… and throws the rock… full force at the boy in the water… hitting him squarely in the head. The boy in the water goes down immediately, and without a word. The father begins to run toward the water, shouting. I look for the boy in the water but do not see him. I run toward the water, and finally, see the boy, face down… and caught in the stream dragging him further toward the center of the river.

Without a thought, I jump, head first into the river and begin swimming toward the boy. The current is strong… much stronger than it looks. I am not making a great deal of progress and see the boy moving further out into the river. I decide to go with the flow of the current, change direction and head directly into the river stream… attempting to cut off the boy as he floats by. I am now maybe fifty yards out into the river, and the current is swift. I momentarily lose sight of the boy and stop, but then see him… maybe twenty yards ahead and further out into the main stream of the river.

Not sure I can get to him before he passes by and is forever lost to the rapid flowing current, I put my head below the water line, and swim harder than ever in my life… as if life depended on it. I see Joyce, Brenda, Kathy… all of them are in the river and I must save them. As I approach the place where the boy should now be, I raise my head and see him, just floating by… I grab, catch his left arm, and hold on.

I've got him, but by now, the current has us both and we are traveling downstream and out of control. I allow the current to take me under its control, while I turn the boy over, and onto his back… I detect no life, and immediately understand that if I don't let him go now, and swim back to shore, then both of us will die.

I hold on, and begin trying to move us back toward shore. We are now, maybe a quarter mile down river and the current is very swift here. I continue to hold the boy, and despite all of the water, see that his head is bleeding, badly… it is a nasty cut. Nothing I can do about that for now. I focus on getting him back to shore. As we continue down river, I see a place up ahead where the river narrows, and there are some trees extending from the edge of the bank. At one spot, there are also bushes hanging over the edge of the river. But, we are too far out... and I am totally out of energy. At this point, the best I am able to accomplish is to hang on to the boy and keep him from drowning (assuming he is still alive).

We are less than 50 feet from the point where the bank and trees protrude and the river narrows. I am now able to see ahead. Immediately after this bank the river widens once again... this is our last chance and I must take it.

Even though I am completely out of strength, I receive some final burst of energy from somewhere... maybe from above, and begin paddling, boy in tow... toward that bank and our last hope for rescue. The current picks up and we must be heading downstream at twenty miles per hour as we pass the river's edge. I have one shot, and as we pass, I grab for a bush... and barely catch it with my left hand.... While still holding the boy with my right arm. I hold on... but I cannot get out of the water... just hold onto the bush branches and wait... until the rest of my energy is gone... *No*, that will not happen.

I hold on for dear life... it seems like hours but is probably less than a minute. I will not let go... I will not let go. I have nothing left. My left arm is aching but that does not bother me. Lately, I've been in constant pain... so what is a little more pain?

The roar of the river is loud, but I begin to hear voices, several of them. They are calling, but I am too weak to respond. I can say nothing... just hang on to the boy and cling to life. I feel a tug, as someone grabs my hand... and literally yanks both me and the boy back onto the bank. I feel my arm pop... but at the same time, feel the earth below me, and know... the boy is safe.

Cloud City

Apparently, they have some very good drugs in the 23rd century. I am in no pain… no pain what so ever. Actually, I am nowhere… and stay there for quite a long time. Days, weeks, months… I can't tell, and I really don't care. Where ever I am… it is a whole lot better than where I was.

But finally, it is time to come home… to face reality… and see what the current *STR* has to offer. I awake and I am not in a bed, but rather, in a soft lounge chair…. Looking out over… wow, it is a view of Earth from the edge of the *SkyCity*… fantastic view. I see the river below… funny, it doesn't look all that dangerous from way up here.

I decide to sit up… big mistake. I am in some sort on mechanical contraption… seems to be wired to several parts of my body. Oh, boy… maybe a 23rd century monster has me in its grips. If so… then go at it… I am done fighting… forever.

I remain relaxed… did I mention the great drugs they have in the 23rd century? Oh, yea, guess I did after all. I am content watching the river below. I am guessing we are a half-mile above the surface… but since I have very few visual reference points, it is just a wild ass guess.

I begin to scan my immediate area… left to right. I see an IV bottle plugged into me… along with some other contraptions… a tube is sticking directly into my stomach. I hope I am not about to give birth to an Alien's baby. Old joke… not funny… well, a little funny, to me at least. I continue to doze… partially awake but mainly in the zone of the 'don't give a shit 'bout anything'.

"How are we feeling today, Jim?" a sweet voice from above asks.

"I don't know about you… but I'm doing pretty damn well… thanks for asking."

"Are you in any pain?"

"Certainly not from this specific incident, I'm not."

"Not sure what that means, but I will take that as a 'NO'."

"Yes… it's a NO," I respond.

"Okay, I believe it's time we cut back on the meds…" the voice from above states.

"Oh shit, I just hate it when that happens," I reply.

"Are you allergic to any medications?" the voice asks.

"A bit late to be asking that question… I've been here…what, a week… ten days."

"Two months, actually… it was touch and go for a while… but you are one hell of a fighter, sorry to be so crude," the voice responds. I am liking her better by the minute.

"How is the boy?" I ask.

"Oh he is fine… they had to aspirate and resuscitate him on the scene… but he is fully recovered, and wants to see you whenever you feel up to it."

"Not sure that is a good idea… just tell him I died… might be simpler than the truth."

"And what is the truth, Mr. Caldwell? …take your time, I have all day."

"Unfortunately, I don't. Could you get me out of these… contraptions, and let me be on my way?"

"Sorry, that won't be possible for a few more days. You are healing well, and we just brought you out of the medically induced coma this morning… so let's give it a few more days, shall we?"

I am no longer liking this female quite so much. "No, let me talk to the doctor… please."

"Oh so you really are from the past… there have not been any doctors for at least sixty years… we have diagnosis equipment… they analyze… they prescribe, we administer."

"And who are 'we'"? I ask.

"I am Pat, a holistic diagnostician."

"Nice to meet you, Pat, I'm James but my friends call me Jim."

"We know who you are. We found your *Keycard* and ran it through our analysis system, and were able to retrieve your records... at least what was left of them. Are you really from the middle 21st century... or was that just a data error... we get a lot of those in our older records."

"Yes, I left home in 2049... and never came back."

"More riddles, Mr. Caldwell... Jim?" Pat inquires.

"I am not into riddles... just facts. Where is my *SmartComm*? I need to know the current *STR* and begin looking for the exit door. If I've already been here two months then I must be close to *Reset.*".

"Excuse me a sec," Pat announces, "*PsychMed* team to the west lounge area... stat."

Well, I certainly know what that means... so decide my talking days are over... as well as my listening days, my caring days... my 'giving a happy horse-shit in hell days'...

...

"Mr. Caldwell... please respond to the questions being asks. We are just trying to determine who you are... where you are from... no one here will hurt you, I promise." This is my fourth day of interrogation, and so far I've kept my promise to myself... have not spoken a single word... to anyone... not even the kitty cat that comes by to visit me every morning.

"We are not giving up on you, Jim," the male voice confirms.

"Only my friends may call me Jim... you may call me Mr. Caldwell... or even Patient X... if you prefer." Oops... I realize I have spoken my first words... and I was hoping to hold out for at least a week... that would be my personal best.

"Well, good... at least that's a start. We have forever, Mr. Caldwell, but from what you told Pat, you may not... since you could be 'reset' at any moment."

What do I look like, the stupidest guy on the planet? He thinks he can bait me... me... the master baiter... oops... that did not come out the way I had planned it. Oh well, it's all in my mind so fuck them... and the *SkyCity* they rode in on.

What's-his-fuck leaves and I am alone once again, so I open my eyes. Still have the IV drip and the feeding tube… well that is certainly an excellent sign…. Ahh, progress.

...

I am now having some pain… guess they really did take me off the pain meds… oh well, I've felt worse… maybe that's their way to try and get me to talk to them… withhold my drugs… boy, they have never seen the likes of me before…

Getting a Grip

I stare out at the green wall for another hour. Yep, they took the nice river view away... guess I was a bad boy... carrot didn't work... so let's try the stick.

"Jim, are you feeling better today?" I detect Pat's voice, and despite my anger that she turned me over to the feds... rather the psych team... and then abandoned me, I am happy to hear her angel-like voice. I decide, however, not to look at her, since she could not be anywhere near as beautiful as she sounds... and I am so easily disappointed.

"Well, it's my old ex-friend Pat... long time no hear."

"Sorry, but once the psych team took over... well, they would not allow me to visit you until their evaluation was complete."

"So when do I get shipped off to the Psych-ward... or whatever it's called in this *STR*."

"You are going to be shipped out... and back into my care... would you like your old room overlooking old Earth... and the river? And, I must have forgotten... what does *STR* mean, again?"

"Clever girl... can't remember... right at the moment... but maybe if I were overlooking the 'old Earth' and assuming my medical coverage is paid up and it covers the upgrade."

"You are and it does. Okay, I'll get you moved ASAP."

"Now, I assume ASAP in medical terms means...anytime in the next ten days?"

"Oh no... we are talking a week... at most." Pat leaves, damn her... and I was just starting to enjoy our bantering...

...

In less than an hour, I am wheeled out of the green room, and taken the several miles back to wherever it was I came from. Interesting. I am not taken in an ambulance or auto, "We haven't had automobiles in over a century", the attendant pushing my wheelchair tells me, I am traveling along some sort of moving sidewalk... fast, smooth... quiet.

Once I arrive, I am taken to a room... but it does have a large window... overlooking... the grounds. "Hey... you promised me a view," I yell, "I want a partial refund..."

I hear the angel's voice, "Now settle down, Jim... or they might return you to psych-ville... and you wouldn't like that, now would you."

"Oh, that wasn't near a bad as some of my more recent experiences... let's say in London 1890... now there's a trip I'll never forget." Not sure why I brought that up... I had long since decided to take that experience to my grave...

"Yes, we will talk all about that... later... but for now we need to get you out of this contraption, as you call it... and get you some food..."

"And wine...? Do you have wine...? They did not have any decent wine in 1890 London... disgusting... how can people live like that?" I offer.

"Not officially... but if you cooperate... I might be able to sneak some in... maybe later tonight."

"For wine... I will agree to marry you and have your baby," I reply.

"That won't be necessary... but thanks for the offer. Now this might hurt a bit, while they are taking out the gastric pump."

"What... are we going into surgery so soon? I just got here..."

"No surgery... it is a simple procedure... we just extract the tube, replace it with a dissolvable plug, and in a few days... you will look almost normal."

"Almost?" I ask.

"Yes, well... you may never look or act *entirely* normal... but I like you anyway."

Not sure what that means... but put it on my short list to things to find out. I watch as a technician arrives, and begins

removing the various apparatus attached to my body. Hurt...
Pain? Are you kidding, it like a small bee sting... almost a tickle,
and I decide to offer that comment, "Oh... that tickles," I state
as I manage a small giggle.

"Jim... you really are weird," Pat responds.

"Thank you," I reply.

It takes less than twenty minutes... and I am device free.
"May I sit up now?" I ask, "or is there, like, a twenty-four hour
period where I must lie perfectly still... not move and not
breathe... else all the stitches will fall out... and we'll have to
start over."

"No, you can get up now, and if you wish... you can
accompany me to the cafeteria... where we can have a meal...
and talk."

"Ah, so is payback going to be a bitch?" I ask.

"We don't use the term 'bitch' in this century... but rather
'strong female'."

"Well... that's a bitch!" I reply.

...

I win round one... or is it round two? Pat helps me to my
feet, and I take my first look at her: "Ahh... 23rd century
monster..." Okay, just kidding. While she is not as beautiful as
Joyce, but then no one is, she is a nice looking thirty plus year
old... well preserved. I've never been into older women... but
then, there is a time and place for everything. We walk the half
mile to the cafeteria. "Really... where are the moving sidewalks
when you need them?" I ask.

"Right over there... but I choose to take the scenic route...
you need the exercise... have you seen yourself in a mirror
lately?" Pat asks.

"No... and I am not looking forward to the experience," I
reply.

We eat cafeteria food... well that hasn't changed much in
the last few hundred year, unfortunately.

Pat has a mature face, a nice smile, and a pleasant
personality. I am not falling in love, (been there, done that, and

137

have the emotional scars to prove it), but I am liking her... being with her is... easy... comfortable... relaxing.

We head back toward my room. It is beginning to get dark out, so I have to ask, "Will the monsters be coming out tonight?"

"Only at the local singles bars," Pat replies without cracking a smile.

"Okay, so can I assume there are no monsters in this *STR*?" I follow-up.

"Oh, I believe *now* would be a good time to talk. We have sort of a local hangout... bar... down the street... it is usually reserved for employees... and their friends. So, for tonight... consider yourself my friend."

Pat takes my hand and leads the way. A 'hangout' is an overstatement or exaggeration ... it is basically a shack with a bar, seats... and lots of folks in blue, red, green, and gold matching outfits. Pat leads me to a seat away from the main bar, a young girl arrives, and Pat orders... two wines. I reach for my *Keycard*... then realize I don't have it with me, "There are no charges here, Jim, consider it your all-inclusive resort."

We sip our drinks, a lot of folks are talking, some rather loud... but most are seemingly enjoying themselves. I think to myself... I want to have fun again... but can I... after what I've been through?

"Okay, now you've got your wine... so no more whining... see what I did there?"

"Is that the best you got?" I reply.

"Oh, no... you ain't' seen nothing, my friend."

"Oh so, 'ain't' is back to being a real word again... if memory serves it was finally removed from the..."

"Shut up and drink your wine... it's my turn to ask the questions. First question... what the fuck is 'STR'?

"And, BTW, the word 'fuck' was never in the official Webster's dictionary... just so you know."

"Not sure who this Webster guy is...but I don't believe I would have liked him a lot."

"Okay...so *STR* stands for 'space-time reference.' The *LifeSim*™ game was created around an almost unlimited number

138

of *STR* points… in order to keep it fresh, unique… and never actually the same, regardless of how many times you play it. And trust me, after almost eleven years of being inside this *Sim*, I can assure you… it is indeed random."

Well, Pat, looks over at me, down at her drink, and then yells, "Jody… scotch please… make it a double."

I decide to enter into this discussion… "Make it two doubles… and the good stuff…"

…

We are well into our second round of… decent…scotch when Pat decides it is now safe to go back into the water… or at least put her toe in it.

"Now," Pat begins, "I do not pretend to understand everything you've told me… but let's see if I got the first part right, okay?"

"Sure, you don't have to be sharpest tool in the shed to be a good person… I get that."

Once again, Pat is staring at me… this time, directly into my soft blue eyes, "Do not make me regret getting you released from solitary confinement. I have the power… and I am not afraid to use it."

I nod, "Please continue… sorry to interrupt."

"What I understand, so far, is you are from a different space-time reference or *STR* as you call it. Is that correct?"

"Yes, I and actually from point Zero, where the *Game* started, you would be in G+200 something… if I could ever find my *SmartComm*…"

"Once again, I must ask you… as politely as I can… 'shut the fuck up and let me ask my question'!"

"Got it," I reply

"So, you are from the past… and from somewhere in the mid-21st century."

"Yes, I left 2049 and entered the *Sim* for the first time… I was conducting the final Beta test before the game went live… but something went wrong…"

"Woo… stop. What is a Sim?"

"A *Sim* is this…" I point all around us, "It is the current… virtual reality… we are in *Sim* 2358: *CloudCity*, and everything here is a *Sim* of that period. We designed it to look and feel real. Most people living here believe they are real, they don't know the difference between *Sim* and *Real*… they live regular lives, just like real people. By now, there were supposed to be thousands of 'real' humans visiting this *STR*, but as I said, before I was so rudely interrupted, something went wrong during the *Beta* test cycle… and I was unable to exit the game… I've been here, inside one of the many *Sims*, ever since." I am done… now I will answer any of Pat's questions.

"One last question, Jim, do you feel that you could make your way back to the Psych ward without assistance… not sure it would be safe accompanying you all that distance… I believe the moon is almost full… and if you start howling… I might panic and try to run… or worse…"

"I'll bet you are cute when you panic?"

"Not so much… just to let you know, I am a black belt Karate… so don't fuck with me." She is no longer smiling, and I suddenly realize that somewhere along the line, I missed the transition boat…. Pat is deadly serious.

"Oh, I thought we were still playing… but I did attempt to answer your questions… as honestly as I could… what part of what I just told you did you not understand?"

"Any of it. I have no idea what an *STR* point is, or a *Sim*… and while I do understand the term 'game'… not in any context you've used, so far."

I look at Pat, and she looks back at me, eyes blinking. I study her face… I can't place her exact model, but she was probably designed… created sometime after I left. I guess we are back to the original Kathy discussion… I assumed she was a *Sim*, part of the *Game*, and acted accordingly.

"Okay, so let me start over, at the basics. First I created this *Game*… or *Sim*… since it is a Virtual Reality model… back in 2048. I created an almost unlimited number of places and times for the game to interact in… with humans, of course. We were getting ready to go live with the game, when my partner, Francis, suggested that I go back one more time, and *Beta* test the environment… just to ensure it was stable, and all of the previous glitches had been resolved. At first I was against the idea, and recommended we go live, and fix anything else that might crop up. We have been testing for almost two years… and never had any major problems."

"Testing what?" Pat asks, again, now appearing somewhat confused.

"I thought that point was clear… the *Game*… testing the game simulation…"

"So… I am beginning to see. You think we are all inside of some game… a game that you invented… do I have that part right?"

Having just recently returned from the psych-ward… I get her train of thought. "Uh, yes, well… let's back away from that for a moment, and maybe come at this from a different direction," I state, now fearing the worse.

"No… *tell me*… are we all inside a game… simulating life… a game that you invented?"

"Now, when you put it that way… a reasonable person might assume that, possibly, I was deranged… and just maybe… A MAD KILLER!"

Pat jumps... she is on her feet and backing away, spilling the rest of her drink on the floor. I thought we were getting somewhere… but it appears I am just another psycho-maniac… might as well play the part. I decide to retreat back into my shell… where it is nice… and warm… and safe.

Time to Give Up?

I awake back in the psych-ward… big surprise there. I am strapped to the bed, and there are several monitors… placed all around me. I see no wires or tubes… so I guess that is a positive sign. But, I must now admit, I am getting really sick and tired of playing this game… I am well past my *Reset* point… so why am I still here?

I am monitored 24/7… for the next six days. I am given certain 'coherency tests', 'environmental reality tests', and something they call a PQ test… I don't ask… they don't tell. I decide to take the tests seriously, understanding that my life, and my freedom may depend on it… at least until my next *Reset* arrives.

Sometime on the sixth day, Pat returns. No smiles, this time, she is all business, "Okay, Jim, you've passed all our tests, so technically, you are considered sane…but you are, obviously, suffering from certain delusions… grand delusions… and those will need to be eliminated… and then you will be free to go."

"Eliminated? I understand you can treat delusions, not that I have any, but how can you eliminate them?"

"Through laser brain surgery… it is actually a very quick and painless procedure. We place this LSC cap on your head, which contains thousands of small and tightly focused lasers. They read and then analyze your brain while the computer asks you a series of questions. As your brain responds to the questions, the laser skull cap, LSC, reads the brain, and adjusts it… removing any damaged or sub-standard tissue, and any other anomalies it may locate during the analysis. Now, of course, no procedure is perfect, but this one is at approximately 90% effective at least 75% of the time."

"Now who's being delusional?" I ask.

"What do you mean? This surgery has been around for almost twenty years… it is well-tested."

"Now, listen to me Pat. First… you will not be cutting into my brain with anything… for any reason! I absolutely forbid it. Now, second, I want you to think about all you just told me… but now assume you were telling this to someone who had just arrived from, let's say, 19th century England. Do you think they would believe you… or would they, possibly, call you delusional and try to lock you up in some psych-ward?"

"Not sure I understand… that does not make sense, Jim… this is state of the art engineering technology based on well-known, tired and proven scientific techniques and principles."

"And so is the *Sim Game* I created back in 2048… and if you don't believe me… then just maybe you should do some research. At the time I invented the VR *Sim Game*… we were in every newspaper in the US. If your online web records go back that far… then search… and you may just find out that I am not as crazy as I may at first appear."

Pat once again looks in my eyes, she is studying me… trying to find the paranoid-schizoid worm that must, by now, be crawling out of at least one of ears or maybe my nose… this time. "Our records of that time are sporadic. The Electronic Pulse War of 2108 wiped quite a few of the online history data banks and archive vaults clean. We restored what we could… but there is no guarantee that any usable data remains from the period you indicate."

"Once again… Electronic Pulse (EP) Wars? I read all about those… in several *Sci-Fi books*.

"Well, of course, we can get a court order authorizing us to perform the surgery even without your consent… but that will take a while, especially since you passed all of the psych tests. Okay, I will research the *v*Web and see what comes up."

"Okay, let me ask this… what is a *v*Web? What does the '*v*' stand for?"

"Virtual, of course… '*v*' is the universal symbol for… oh I get it. We have a virtual web… and you created a virtual game. Okay, if that is the case… then where is your game… why have

I never heard of it…. Was it, possibly, so bad, that all records of its very existence were destroyed?"

"I hope so," I respond, using my totally serious expression. "I truly wish I had never created it… and if I had it to do over, you can bet your sweet ass I would destroy all records assoc… uhhh… maybe that is what happened… maybe I finally made it back to 2050… and decided to completely destroy the game and erase every trace of it?"

"Now, it's your time to look in the mirror and tell me what you see… are you so powerful that you can destroy all evidence that your supposed game ever existed… or is that another of your delusions… think rationally, Jim… most of what you've told me… told us… is impossible… or at least highly improbable."

"Gotcha! Highly improbable means you must prove, to a level of reasonable certainty, that it does not exist… so… go off and prove it… but, please, don't put me back in those restraints. I promise not to leave. Remember, I came back with you voluntarily… you did not hold a gun to my head?'

"What's a 'gun?" Pat asks.

"Probably just another of my delusions. If you don't understand something… let's call it a delusion… and move on."

...

Pat confers with her colleagues, and they decide not to restrain me… but I must remain on the psych ward until this is cleared up… one way or the other.

I have no idea where my *SmartComm* is… and that worries me. I really don't use it for much… but it has a record of all my travels… place, time, dates, and even some of the key events… but only those I chose to enter… and that does not include the details of my visit with Brenda.

It is another 48 hours before I hear back from Pat. She arrives, unannounced, and states," Let's head down to the conference room… and chat." I follow her, and once we are seated, I decide to bring out the old Jim… and try him on for size once again, "What, no wine? Sorry but I cannot have any serious discussion without a few glasses of wine."

"I can't get wine in here?"

"Can't or won't?" I reply, using my stubborn brat voice, which, BTW, I'm damn good at.

Pat presses a couple of buttons on her watch and then speaks, "Bring a bottle of chilled wine, and two glasses down to conference room B... stat."

"You heard me... stat!"

"Now, let's talk," Pat begins.

"Not until the wine arrives... no wine... no talk," I state.

"You can be such a bastard..."

"Watch out now... I can slang with the best of them, trust me sister, you do not want to get into a pissing contest with me!"

We wait, and it is at least twenty minutes before the wine arrives. "You will need to sign for this Pat... and once the Super finds out... you just might be in deep shit," the attendant expresses, as he drops the wine and glasses, receives his signature and leaves.

"Ohhh. Hope I didn't get you in any trouble?" I begin, "But if I did... I'm sure there is some laser brain surgery that will cure you... make you forget I ever existed," I state, quite pleased with myself.

"If only." She replies.

"They forgot the cork screw," I state. "That's okay... I can probably twist it out with my teeth... that's how bad I need a glass of wine."

"I'll bet you can... but no need for such drastic measures." Pat picks up the bottle and presses down on the top of the cork... and out it comes... slowly. She removes it from the bottle, and pours us both drinks.

"What, no ice? Well that is just uncivilized," I express, but quickly grab the half full glass and drink it down.

"You keep pushing my buttons... why is that?" Pat questions.

"Pushing your buttons? Have I ever, in recent memory, threatened to cut out a section of your brain?" I ask.

"Okay... let's stop... I concede... you win the round... game and match... can we please move on to the topic at hand. BTW, this communication is being recorded... officially for the record... do you consent to this video record."

"Fuck you!" I reply.

"I'll take that as a 'Yes'."

...

We drink in silence, for a while... I believe I've gotten it out of my system, but cannot be sure until Pat begins to talk again... her voice used to sound like an angel... whatever happened to that Pat... oh yea, she turned into Royal Bitch Pat... now I remember.

"Okay, Jim, let's begin again," Pat restarts the conversation, and this time she is talking barely above a whisper, "I did a lot of research on your... Sim *Game*... but could not find a single reference to it... anywhere. Honestly, I tried dozens of variables... but got not a single hit."

"If that is the case, then why am I not in restraints right now, instead of here sipping wine with you?"

"Because, I found this..."

2057.03.17.21:18:06 LA Times

It was announced today by the LA coroner's office, that James Kirkland Caldwell, 32, from Pasadena, CA, has officially been declared dead. If you will remember, almost ten years ago, Dr. Caldwell invented the *FgU* VR Simulation Game, which was, reportedly, a revolutionary breakthrough in Virtual Reality and simulation modeling technology. Unfortunately, just weeks prior to the delivery of the first one million pre-ordered units of the software, Dr. Caldwell disappeared... and has never been heard from again.

His business partner and life-long friend, Francis Jamison, had this to say, "Jim insisted on testing the software one last time. He, apparently, went into the *Sim Beta* mode... and was never seen again. We will miss, you, buddy!"

According to the coroner report, "Since the seven year statutory limitation has been reached, we are officially declaring James Caldwell... as deceased." As was expected, his longtime business partner, Mr. Jamison, will inherit all of Dr. Caldwell's assets, which are currently estimated to exceed Two Billion Credits. Dr. Caldwell had no other family and has never been married. There will not be a memorial service.

I read the article twice, and then look up at Pat, "What, no memorial service? I gave them the best years of my life... and that's the thanks I get?"

"All I want to know, Jim... *is that you*? Now before you answer I must advise that as part of the video recording... your brain waves are being analyzed in terms of what you say being True, being False, or being Questionable... do you understand?"

"At least I still have brain waves... no thanks to you," I respond. "But, to answer your question... for the record... yes... I am Dr. James Caldwell."

Despite my response to Pat... inside, I am devastated... declared dead... and my partner gets my assets... I didn't have a will... why should I? I was only 23 when I invented the VR *Sim Game*... who even thinks of a will at 23?

"Jim, are you still with us?" Pat asks.

"Where the fuck else would I be?" I respond, and detect just a hint of anger creeping back into my voice... well maybe more than a hint.

"Yea, I believe I understand how you might be feeling," Pat states, and sorry, but I cannot let that one pass.

"Oh you do...? Did you spend the last ten years in a Sim, being eaten by monsters, watching as the only girl you've ever truly loved faded out of existence... while looking at the remains of her best friend... who's various body parts were scattered across the floor, and walls of your hotel room... did you do that, Pat?"

"No, Jim... I did not. I am truly sorry for your loss... but we still have not proven you are totally sane. I am convinced... but I'm not sure a court will be. We must come up with some other proof...."

"Yea, well, if I hadn't lost my *SmartComm*, we could download the data... from my various... adventures... and that would collaborate my story."

"Oh, we have your *SmartComm*. It is safely locked away along with your Universal *Keycard*... we could never figure out how you came to possess an unlimited credit universal key card... but it authenticated..."

"Yea, well being worth a few billion or so… has its perks, I guess."

"So you really are Dr. James Caldwell?" Pat asks.

"Yes, I am Dr. Caldwell… but my friends call me Jim. Pat, are you my friend?" I ask.

"I hope so, Jim… I really want to be your friend."

Seeing the Big Picture

I remain confined to the psych-ward for another week, but Pat comes by every day, takes me out for a walk around the grounds. We stop, and look out over the edge of *CloudCity*... and then we head out for drinks. That last part is always unauthorized... but that is the part I appreciate the most.

We get the official ruling which is, "Sanity confirmed... no LSC required... case dismissed." Apparently, I am a free man.

Pat drops by with the paperwork, I sign her *slate*, and I am free to leave. "What now?" Pat asks.

"I wait," I reply.

"Wait for what?" she asks.

"For the *Reset*... this has been the longest time I've ever spent in a *STR* before. I don't understand why I am still here... but the time does vary, based on an algorithm I wrote way back in college... but never mind that bit of trivia. I'll just leave now... you've done quite enough... I'm used to making it on my own... I have a great deal of practice."

"Have you ever considered the possibility... however slim that possibility might be, that just maybe, this is not part of the *Sim Game* you created... but is... its own reality. We exist, we are real... we are not *Sims*?"

"Yes, I have considered that. And if that is indeed the case... then I am certainly insane... and I cannot admit that I am insane."

"Why?" Pat replies.

"Why can't I admit I'm insane?" I ask.

"No, why must you be insane if this is a reality and not part of your *Sim* game... have you even considered that possibility?"

"NO, I have not. How could it be? For almost eleven years, I've moved from *STR to STR*... I've been back as far as the 1700s... dim times... I would not recommend them. I have been forward as far as... well 2353."

"Do you see any difference between this *STR*, and the other's you've visited?"

"You mean other than no monsters... not really... the Sims here are the best I've ever seen, but I assume the technology has improved since I left 2049."

"Is there anyway... any way at all, that you could consider me as real and not a Sim?"

"Yes, I have met several others, during my journey, who were real... but even they knew they were inside a *Sim*... you are the first person I've met, who believes they are real, but are not somehow trapped inside this *Sim*."

"Jim, I've lived here all my life... for almost 50 years... and I remember almost every moment," Pat states.

I look at Pat... "You are... fifty?"

"Yes, I'll be 51 in September... does that surprise you?"

"Well, yes it does... I was guessing maybe 35."

"We have lots of advanced anti-aging techniques, plus there is no pollution... we conquered global warming... cancer is gone... all of it. The average person lives to be about 150... some reach 200."

"Good to know. If I were looking for a home, then I would consider staying here... but there are people back in the past, who I need to find. A female named Joyce, who I now know I love, and a man named Francis, who I now suspect betrayed me... maybe even caused my death."

"But, you are not dead, Jim... you are alive, and living in the mid-23rd century. If you could only accept that fact... then maybe your life would improve, things would begin to change, and you could be happy again.

"Thanks again... but I don't believe any of it... so will find the closest hotel... get the biggest room available... and drink as much scotch as I can possibly consume, until the *Reset* occurs."

Nothing like a dramatic exit... and with that said, I walk out of the hospital, or what-ever-the-hell this place is, and head for town.

...

It takes less than two hours to reach the center of the *City*, but I remain badly out of shape and, not only are my feet wobbly from lack of recent exercise, but every part of my body is aching... tingling... or burning. I've passed a couple of decent looking hotels, but, as I informed Pat, I am holding out for the Penthouse suite at the Ritz... or as close as I can get.

Finally, up ahead I see the tower. It is magnificent, tall, slim, gleaming. The entire building seems to cast a soft blue light... that appears to be coming from the building itself. It attracts me like a lightening bug to light. I walk directly to the main entrance, the doors disappear, and I am standing in the main lobby. The lobby ceiling must be a hundred feet high. The lobby is very ornate... out of character for this high tech *SkyCity*... and it looks much larger than the entire outside of the building... this is definitely *VR*. Pat almost had me convinced this was real... but a *VR* hotel... I rest my case. I head to the front desk. "A room please... I mean the largest suite you have available... top floor, if that is available."

"Sir, our availability is quite limited... do you have a reservation?"

"Yes, I do," I state as I throw my *Keycard* on the counter. The desk clerk picks up the card, does not wink, but does head over the registration machine, slide in the card... and I see the green light flashing.

He returns, "Yes, sir, we have several large suites available... but unfortunately, the Presidential Suite is taken."

"Oh, such a pity," I feign, "But... okay... just do the best you can."

"I can get you on the top floor... and with a nice view of the City... will that work?"

"How large... I really need a large suite... I expect to entertain lots of folks while I'm here," I lie.

"Well, it's not our largest, let me check... about 2000 square feet, three bedrooms, a fully stocked bar... gaming room, gambling room... full kitchen... also stocked with food... beverages... will that be sufficient... Sir?"

"Yes, that will work."

"Excellent, I will have the bell-boy retrieve your luggage."

"No need... I am packing light... plan to buy everything I need... right here in town. Now, one last thing... could you point me to the nearest bar... I would like a few refreshments prior to retiring to my room."

"Certainly... there are two main bars... one across the way... over there, and the other is at the top of the hotel... 51st floor. Just insert your card in the elevator slot, and press BAR. When you are ready to visit your room, then press PENTHOUSE. Is there anything else, sir?"

"No, that will do it... room key please."

"Oh, just use your universal *Keycard*, in the elevator, and to gain access to your room... we are fully FT17 certified. Have a wonderful stay, and let me know personally if you need anything," He hands me his card. "I work 7AM to 4PM, so after that... just contact the clerk on duty, and he or she will assist you."

...

I am liking this *City* better already. I head to the elevator, insert my card and Press BAR. The elevator door opens... wow... 51st floor... now that was quick. I enter the most beautiful bar I have ever seen. The view is 360 degrees... no matter where you are... the city is all around you. Now, I've programmed VR effects for years... but have never seen anything this clever before. It must be an optical illusion... I will have to ask. I decide to sit at the main bar... and as I walk toward the bar it begins to expand in front of me, a seat is available and I am 'directed' toward it. The seat slides to the side, and as I walk into it, I feel the seat fold around me... embrace me. I feels like leather, it adjusts to my body. I relax.

"Yes, sir, what can I get for you?" A lovely voice asks, and I look up. She is cute... maybe 25, long yellowish-blond hair down to her waist, and the most beautiful olive complexion I've ever seen.

"A 15-year-old scotch... if you have one," I state, remaining in my snotty-snobbish persona, at least for now.

"We have several of those to choose from, but you may want to consider our 25-year-old scotch, if price is no object."

"Sounds good, let me have a double... on the rocks, please." I reach for my *Keycard*, but the bartender shakes her head.

"We have the proximity sensors up here... your card has already been scanned... and an unlimited purchase limit has been pre-authorized... welcome to the Regency International Hotel, sir."

Living like There is No Tomorrow

After all of the shit, hell, and mental/physical abuse I've had to endure over these last eleven years... I decide I will take this opportunity to exploit the good side of VR... *Sim.* Now, I would not want to mislead you... I've had several good experiences over these last eleven years... but honestly, most of them end in tragedy... well... it's the way we designed the game. Remember those in-app add-ons we discussed earlier... well, they work best when you have a bad experience, and want to *Reset*, undo, or redeem yourself... it's just marketing... nothing personal.

"So, does it live up to your expectations?" the bartender asks.

"Oh, yea... It is... without a doubt, the best scotch I've ever had... and trust me... I've had a lot of scotch in my lifetime. I'm Jim, what's your name?"

"I'm Jasmine. Nice to meet you." She actually extends her hand and we shake. "Bill and I will be taking care of you this afternoon... let either of us know if you need anything... enjoy your drink."

I have not seen another bartender, but then, my virtual bar is only about eight feet wide... and the rest is a view of the city... a 360 degree view. I look behind me, but all I see is view... is there anyone else in the bar. A gentleman enters my view, "Excuse me, sir, am I the only one in the bar today?" I ask.

"No, sir, we are almost at capacity... but the default setting is 'single view mode'. If you would like I can easily change that setting."

"Not sure what that means... this is my first time..."

"Oh, of course… we have the most advanced VR system in the City. Most all bars and restaurants, and entertainment centers have VR… but we take it to the extreme… that's what makes us different… unique. Shall I change the setting?"

"What are my choices?" I ask.

"You are in single mode… we can do family mode… area mode… or all inclusive."

"Let's try 'all inclusive'." I state.

"Yes, sir," the bartender pulls out a small remote, points it at me, and presses a button…. I am overwhelmed… there are hundreds of people in the bar… it is loud… they are everywhere… but, for some indefinable reason… this makes me happy.

"Will that work for you, sir?" the bartender asks.

"Yes, that will work," I state, as I look around and see all of the folks apparently having a great time in the bar. Can all of these folks be *Sims*, I have to ask myself… and does that even make sense? Of course, we program every environment with a variety of *Sims*, so the humans will not feel alone… and it will appear to be a normal setting… but this place is packed… folks are loud, people are walking around with drinks in hand… some are even acting obnoxious… just like real humans often do.

…

I can now see the entire bar. It must be sixty feet long. Jasmine and Bill are both hustling… serving drinks… talking to customers. I watch for a minute… something seems different here. They are not as coordinated as I would have programmed. They keep getting into each other's way. They stop, back up… Jasmine even spills a portion of a drink she has just mixed… I would never allow that in one of my *Sims*.

Jasmine spots me looking at her, and rushes over, "Would you like another, James?"

"I am fine for now… just watching the two of you interact."

"Oh, sorry about that… it's Bill's second night bartending… and we have not yet coordinated our act. He is a good bartender... but it takes time to get the timing and rhythm correct... you understand."

"Certainly," I reply, "And yes, one more before I go... then cash me out."

I watch as Jasmine heads to the other end of the bar, reaches high up into the cabinet, retrieves a bottle... I've never seen that bottle design before, and pours a double, adds a few ice cubes, and returns with the drink.

"Thank you, can you check me out... and add a 25% tip for yourself," I tell Jasmine once the drink arrives.

"Much appreciated... and I hope to see you back here soon... are you staying at the hotel?"

"Yes, I'll be here... maybe for a while."

"Good, please come back when we are not so busy... and have a moment to chat... have a great evening."

The official receipt dissolves into existence in front of me. I verify the tip has been added, and press ACCEPT, using my thumb. The receipt turns green and then slowly dissolves out of existence.

I finish my drink and think... What a nice day... for a change. No responsibilities... no duties to perform... no one to save from impending peril. I can get use to this.

I head back to the elevator and press PENTHOUSE... and I am inside my suite. How did that happen? I look around... damn this is one huge suite. I try to find the VR effects... but I am unable... everything looks real. Again, the overall concept is ornate... maybe eighteenth or nineteenth century motif... but that is coupled with the latest in 23rd century technology. I head to the kitchen, and as I approach, a bottle slides out of the cabinet. In my mind I hear, "Would you care for a scotch?" So, they have a learning system, as well... impressive.

"Not at this time," I respond. The bottle recedes back into the cabinet.

I open the refrigerator, see a bottle of water, retrieve it and drink. I need to eat, so head over to the center aisle, there is food, cheese... meats, bread... I make sandwiches....

The food is excellent... doesn't taste at all like synthetic food... wow, they really have improved the process. I decide to stroll around my suite… it is the size of a small home… not as large as my home back in 2050, but for a hotel suite… huge. I spot the balcony and as I approach, the door slides open and I enter the deck. Where before it was quiet, I now hear the noises of the *City*. No cars, trucks, or police sirens… but other noises. I look down… thousands of folks are traveling along the various sidewalks. Some are walking, some jogging, but most are standing still, allowing the sidewalk to move them to their destination. I hear the people walking, talking, I head birds signing, and the general flow of life below. For now… I am content.

It is pleasant out, maybe 70 degrees, low humidity, with a few fluffy clouds in the sky. I decide to remain outside and hopefully, watch the sunset. Given the state of VR effects in this *STR*, I except to see a spectacular sunset and afterglow. I decide to head back in, bring out the scotch bottle, a glass, and some ice, and remain here until after the sun sets.

…

I remain fascinated with this city. It looks to be, possibly, ten miles long and at least two miles wide… and there appears to be some sort of layering effect. I see folks taking moving sidewalks underground… and make a mental note to try that for myself… and see where those paths lead. I surmise that there might be an underground mass transit system, allowing folks to quickly reach the extremities of *CloudCity*. I'll check it out tomorrow.

As I stroll around the huge balcony, which wraps around two sides of the building (another VR illusion, I assume), I spot the park below. I did not see that on my way in earlier. Looks to be maybe twice the size of NYC Central Park of my day, and it too has rivers, lakes, children's play areas, park benches, and more. I add that to my 'to do' list.

Finally, the sun begins to set. I return to my comfy lounge chair, pour myself a final scotch, and watch as the sun sets behind the buildings toward the other end of the City. The reflections of the sun against the buildings reminds me of watching a San Francisco sunset from the Sausalito side, but without all of the pollution (we still have global warming issues in 2050… which is even another reason I know this is a *Sim*.)

Other than the reflection from the buildings, the sunset is a major disappointment. Once the sun sets, the stars come out almost immediately, and there is zero afterglow. Maybe I'll discuss that with the front desk clerk… and see when the next afterglow is scheduled.

Once the stars are out… and damn they are clear and bright… the temperature begins to fall quickly, and a strong breeze arrives from the west. Time to go inside…

As I return from the balcony, lights start coming on throughout the suite. Low, dim lights… some are in the walls and others in the ceiling. As I approach a section of the suite, the lights ahead glow brighter, and the lights behind dim back to their original setting. While we have panel lights in 2050… these are much more subtle and integrated into the suite itself… but then I remember the VR effect, and I'm not quite so impressed as before.

I place the now half-full scotch bottle on the counter, and watch as it slides back into the cabinet. I place the glass in the sink, and it quickly disappears. It is barely eight PM and I am already bored. My anticipation was to return to my 'bad boy' persona, and wreak havoc over the *City*… taking my revenge for what this *Game* has done to me, and the ones I loved. However, as of right now, at least… I am relatively happy and somewhat content. I decide to head to bed… get some sleep… and then see what tomorrow brings.

…

I awake to the sound of a soft bell; ding…… ding….. ding. I look around and see the communication device on the table glowing… must be the front desk. I walk over, press talk/view, and Pat is staring at me, "Just checking to see how you were getting along. Looks like you found the right hotel… are you enjoying it?"

"Yes, I am… and thanks for asking… but… how did you know I was here?"

"Oh, easy, since you are a visitor here and not a resident, we use your *Keycard* to track your location… and we are allowed to check in with you every so often. I would have mentioned that yesterday, but you were in such a hurry to leave… that I decided it could wait."

"Oh, okay… thought maybe you missed me… should have known it was a business call?"

"I do miss you, Jim… and this is not a business call. You left in a state of agitation, and I wanted to ensure that you got what you needed and was on the road to… maybe feeling a bit better about… things."

"Yes, I am. The hotel is nice, the folks are friendly, and the VR effects are the best I've seen."

"Good to know. Now, this is not a police state, so if you don't want to be tracked, or for me to ever contact you again, I will place the call in record mode, you can tell me, and the trace will be immediately deactivated."

"Will anyone but you be contacting me?" I inquire.

"No, only me."

"Then you can keep the trace… it's actually good to hear from you… and you are welcome to contact me again… if you so desire."

"Good… I'll do that… one more thing, if you need to contact me… I did link my personal Comm to your *SmartComm*… so look under 'Friends', 'Pat'… that's me. And if it's acceptable, any future *Comms* will be via your *SmartComm*."

Hum, interesting. "That works for me… thanks Pat… have a nice day." I disconnect and think. I do like Pat… maybe not as a potential lover… but just maybe, as a friend.

Tomorrow

I'm now been on my on in *CloudCity* for almost a full week… since I left the "institute". Pat's called twice, but each conversation has been short, and she has not suggested we meet for drinks or dinner… and I don't believe I will be taking the lead on any relationship that might come about between the two of us.

I am still waiting for the *Reset* to occur. Including my two months in the medically induced coma, I've now been in this *STR* for close to three months… the longest ever in a single *STR*. I decide to head back up to the Top Floor Bar, and hope Jasmine is working today. I still don't understand the whole on shift/off shift thing… maybe that was designed to mix things up… provide better variety.

I've been back to this bar three times, but Jasmine was working only once, and they were slammed. I am attempting to find her at the bar on a day that is not so busy, so we can talk. No, I do not want to get into her cute little panties… although I'm certain that would be a wonderful and breathtaking experience. Usually, it's the bartender who gives you the straight scoop… provides the vital information required to assist you in planning your day, week… however long I might have in a specific *STR*.

Jasmine is working, and the bar is less than half full. I spot another male bartender, but it is not Bill. Jasmine spots me, heads toward the 'special' scotch, pours a generous double, and smiles as she sets the glass in front of me. "Jim… been a while… I thought you had abandoned me," she starts, face all a glow.

"Never… but you don't seem to be working a lot this last week, at least not on the days and times I've been coming by." I lead… hoping to get some new information.

"My schedule is… flexible since I am still attending college full time. I work mostly at nights and anytime on the weekends."

Great cover story, I think to myself, "So where is Bill…? I haven't seen him either."

"Oh, Bill didn't make the cut… they let him go Tuesday night… he was just too slow for this crowd… he was a nice guy… but 'Biz' is 'Biz'."

A *Sim* being fired… is that even possible? Must be part of a very sophisticated scenario designed to achieve… what? I sip my scotch as I watch Jasmine wait on other customer. While she appears friendly and courteous to everyone… she does seem to spend more time with me… and is extremely friendly… but then I chalk that up to being a huge tipper… 25% of a hundred credit tab for three scotches… pretty generous.

I decide I need to get to know Jasmine… away from this bar. She may end up being my primary information source… since Pat never tells me anything… mostly asks me questions… and that does me no good, at all.

I finish my second double, and wave as she looks my way. I've noticed that the crowd had died down quite a bit since my arrival. The other bartender seems to be handling the current traffic… so maybe now is a good time to talk.

"You ready for another, Jim?" Jasmine asks, as she smiles at me.

"Yes, but can we talk some, as well… I see you are not quite a busy as before…"

"Certainly, things are beginning to slow down. As a matter of fact, I was taking to Frank about leaving early… so, why don't we move to a table… have a few drinks… and talk?"

"Excellent… I would love that. Get us both a drink, and I'll move over to that back table… if that is okay?"

"Sure, give me five minutes to check out… and get the drinks."

I move about as far away from the bar as is possible. Take a table next to a window overlooking the City. Can't tell if it's real or virtual... and don't really care at this point... nice view. Jasmine arrives and sets the two drinks on the table.

"So what are you drinking?" I ask, just to open the conversation.

"Oh, I'm a scotch drinker, also, but certainly not the good stuff that you drink... I have to settle for the eight year old kind... but still not bad."

"Excuse me... I'll be right back," I state as I get up from the table, pick up her glass, and head back to the bar. The male bartender is nowhere in sight, so I decide to go behind the bar, pick up the best double rocks glass I can find, reach up into the cabinet, get the good scotch, and pour a nice double. Since her original drink had no ice, I pour this one neat, as well. I leave the bottle on the counter and return to the table.

As I place her drink on the table, I state, "When you drink with me... you drink only the best."

"Wow, Jim... thank you... I've never even tried the 25 year old stuff, at thirty-five credits a pop... I would probably be fired." She stops, looks at me, then the scotch, and takes a test sip. Her face lights, "Damn that is some good shit, oh sorry... I am not supposed to curse in front of the customers."

"When we are drinking together, please, consider me a friend... and not a customer."

"Okay, here's to friendship," we toast and drink. "Damn good... smooth..." she states.

I start slow, asking very general questions, really just getting to know her. I have no agenda. I am truly enjoying sitting here with Jasmine... she is sweet, kind, and a little funny... at times.

"I can tell you are not from around here, Jim... do you live in one of the alternate worlds?"

I almost spit out my drink, but quickly recover... "Define alternate worlds?" I ask.

"Oh, you know, the other *SkyCites* located around the Earth... we locals call them 'alternate worlds'... it's just slang, hope I didn't offend you."

"No offense taken, and yes, I am not from *CloudCity*. I got here a couple of months ago... and do expect to leave, at any time now."

"Oh, that's a shame... I thought we might get to know each other a little better."

"That is exactly what we are doing... right now," I respond.

"So, when do you leave?"

"Unknown... I'm kind of on a day-to-day basis... could be a day... week... who knows."

"Hope it's a month," Jasmine replies, and once again, smiles. After three double scotches, neither of us is filling any pain, but I decide it is past time to eat.

"Can I invite you to dinner... here or anywhere you wish to go?"

"Here is fine... if that is okay. I like you a lot, Jim... but let's take it slow... if that is okay?"

I look into Jasmine's eyes, and for the first time... I *want* her. Sorry Joyce, but life moves on... or you die... or in my case... both.

"Oh, I agree... let's not start something we can't possibly finish. But let's have dinner together, at least... I am having a wonderful time."

"Me too... let's order... the steaks here are excellent, the fish is fresh caught in the river below or the ocean... flown in daily. I would not recommend the 'Rack of Lamb' or the 'Fried Duck'... but most anything else is good."

"And what are you ordering?" I ask.

"Oh, just a Caesar salad for me... I'm dieting," Jasmine replies, and I am not able to read her face on this one.

"Sorry... but that doesn't work for me. I want the steak... the largest they have... so, please, will you reconsider and eat something substantial... you do not need to lose an ounce... that is for certain."

"Okay, well, thanks, I'll have the steak as well."

Since we are out of the bar area, and into the restaurant section, a waiter eventually arrives to take our order. "I see you have your drinks... what can I get you to eat?" he asks. I am not impressed with this guy, but do not want to cause a scene... not on my first date with Jasmine.

Jasmine orders the filet, medium, side Caesar salad, and the garden veggies.

"I'll have the same, except, instead of the filet, make that a New York strip."

"Any your sides?" he asks.

"Were you not listening?" I ask, for some reason, I'm starting to get a bit perturbed with our waiter.

"Frankie!" Jasmine steps in... "Cut the shit... make his exactly like mine except sub the strip for the filet... now go..."

The waiter... Frankie, leaves, "And what is his problem?" I ask.

"Oh Frankie is not a bad guy... but his girlfriend just dumped him... and he seems a bit distracted lately... I'll talk to him... let's not let it ruin our evening, okay?" Jasmine insists.

"Nothing could ruin this evening... and I will now back away from even thinking about Frankie... I had rather be thinking about ... you."

Tonight

Frankie is MIA and finally, Jasmine heads back to the kitchen, and returns with our meals, "Sorry, but apparently Frankie did not appreciate our attitude... and quit. No matter, here is our food... let's enjoy."

The meal is excellent, best I've ever had in a *Sim* before. I want desert, but since Jasmine declines, then so do I. We do decide on coffee... "It is French press and the best in town," she assures me.

It is wonderful, and I begin to sober up... but not so much that I no longer want Jasmine... but we've agreed... take it slow. It is almost midnight when we leave the restaurant. "Do you need me to walk you home?" I ask.

"No, that won't be necessary... but thank you for a wonderful evening, and I hope to see you again... soon." We are standing next to the elevator waiting for its arrival, when Jasmine takes my hand, I look over at her, and we kiss. At first it's a soft kiss, but we cannot seem to stop... and our kiss becomes intensive, passionate... wanting. We finally break, as the elevator arrives, we enter, she presses Lobby and I press Penthouse. The door closes, and I am in my suite. Slightly depressed... but, at the same time feeling wonderful.

I turn toward my bedroom, and begin to remove my shirt, when I hear a soft knock on the door. I turn and open the door... and there is Jasmine. We say nothing, I let her in, we kiss, and slowly head into the bedroom.

...

I awake, it is light out, and Jasmine is right there, beside me, cuddling. God, I think, I must have this woman again. I turn to face her, she opens one eye, smiles, and we make love again.

…

It is almost noon before we finally get out of bed. "Let's go to brunch, I offer… it's Saturday or Sunday… I believe," I suggest, not really keeping track of the days of the week… or the weeks of the year, for that matter.

"I should be getting back home… really… but okay… brunch it is. There is a jazz brunch right down the street from here… I'll call for reservations…"

I get up, take my shower, dress, and head into the kitchen. Jasmine is not there, but the coffee is brewing, so I help myself. Not as good as the French press… but it will do… I take a seat at the small kitchen table, and sip my coffee, deeply lost in thought. I am in the process of rethinking… everything, when Jasmine comes out of the bedroom, "Sorry, to be wearing the same outfit as yesterday… but you know… shit happens!"

I find that to be extremely funny, and break out in a laugh, and Jasmine joins me. She gets her coffee and joins me. "Our reservations are in one hour… if that is okay?"

"Perfect… do you have any certain time you must be home… or back to work?" I ask.

"No, not today… I canceled my only… appointment, so I'm free all day."

"Good, then please spend it with me… all of it… every minute!"

"Sounds like a plan," Jasmine responds.

…

The jazz brunch is, well… wonderful… delicious… good music… excellent champagne… on a scale of ten… I guess I would rate it an eleven. The extra point is for being in the company of Jasmine.

167

"Where to next?" I ask as we are leaving the Jazz brunch, hand in hand.

"Anywhere you want, Jim… as far as I'm concerned… I never want this day to end…"

I ask Jasmine if she would mind giving me a brief tour of the city… just the highlights… focal points… She agrees and we begin our walk around town. We spend the next three hours, walking, touring, visiting, enjoying. I love the park… we walk from end to end and that takes almost an hour. Toward the far end of the park, we decide to take a breather, and locate a nice park bench under a large oak tree.

"We need to talk," Jasmine states.

"Oh, shit… I knew this was too good to be true," I reply.

"No, it's not that… it's exactly the opposite. I believe I am already in love with you, Jim. I know that is not logically… but that is what I am feeling."

"And when has love ever been logical?" I ask.

"Good point… sometimes a huge mistake… but seldom logical," she replies.

I fall back into thought… attempting to balance the overall equation. My mind is absorbing all of this information… these emotions… and my internal alarm is sounding… big time. How can I possibly fall in love with a *Sim.* The answer is, simply… I cannot.

Therefore, Jasmine is not a Sim… Jasmine must be a real human being.

"Jim… where are you?" Jasmine shouts, and I awake. "Sorry, I was just thinking…" I reply.

"About what?"

"Can we go back to my suite and talk… for a long time… maybe the rest of today… tomorrow… can we?"

"Absolutely… we can talk for a long as you want… let's go."

We walk hand in hand back to the hotel. It is a beautiful City… too good to be real… but I am beginning to believe that it is real, and not a Sim after all. How can that possibly be? I have no idea. But, I now must find out. This becomes my new mission… Is *CloudCity* real, and if so… how and why?

Reality or Sim... Is There a Difference?

We arrive back at the hotel, but Jasmine states, "I do need to return home and get some clothes... personal accessories... you understand?"

"I really don't want you to do that... to leave me now... there are shops right here...purchase anything and everything you heart desires... I will pay... no commitments... no obligation... I just do not want you to leave me."

Jasmine stops, drops my hand and looks into my face. "This is huge, Jim... but something here is not right... the equation is out of balance... and I don't understand exactly what is happening between us. I do not want to leave you either, and I will do as you suggest... but once we are back in your suite... we must have a very serious conversation, and get to the bottom of this, whatever *this* is. We must tell each other the truth... the whole truth... and nothing but the truth, agreed?"

"Agreed, but, just promise me this... no matter how strange my tale appears... it will be the honest truth... so please do not run away. If you feel toward me the way I feel toward you... we need to stand and fight for each other... and not run away."

"I'm never run away from anything in my life, Jim, and I do not intend to start now!"

...

Jasmine purchases a few items, clothing outfits, personal accessories... and a few other things she might need. I never look at the bottom line, just press my thumb where indicated… the green light flashes, and we are on our way.

We have just arrived back in the suite, when there is knock at the door. I open, and the waiter is there with the afternoon snacks, wine, and small candies for deserts.

"I could get used to living like this," Jasmine states as she snacks on some of the cheeses, and I pour the wine.

"Then get used to it…" I reply.

"Okay so let's begin that talk… and here is my first question… assuming you are ready for this?"

"Bring it one," I reply.

"How in hell do you have an unlimited Credit *Keycard?* I have never heard or seen anything like that, but every time you enter the bar… the priority light flashes, and the screens shows 'No limit Account'. What does that even mean?"

"Well, until earlier today, I thought it had the answer to that question, but now, I'm no longer certain. I told you I would tell you the truth, and I will, but before, when I've done that, I was locked up in the local insane asylum… and it took me a while to get out."

Jasmine sips her wine, eats another cube of cheese… "I can see that… proceed."

"Well, as I stated earlier… I am not from *here.* But, I alluded that I was from one of the alternative worlds… well the world I'm from can certainly be classified as 'alternative'."

"Okay, you've got my interest, but I am not yet sacred… I understand you are different… a one of kind… I get that… continue."

"Okay. Here it is. I am not from this time at all… I am from your past. I left Earth, as we know it, right around 2050… and I've spend the last eleven years in the past… in the future and in limbo."

"Okay… well maybe I'm a little scared."

"But, that not the worst of it."

"Oh, it gets worse than being from the past *and* the future?" Jasmine asks.

"Yes. I have spent the last eleven years inside a simulated video game, a *Sim* game I invented, moving from *STR* to *STR*. Now, if you wish to leave, I will understand... believe me.

"Not yet, but getting close," she responds, as she glances sideways, locates the exit... and mentally plans her escape route.

I decide to take a deep breath before continuing. "Back in 2048 I invented this game, called *LifeSim™*. But, let me backtrack just a bit from that. I received my first PhD when I was nineteen. They all called me a boy genius... a prodigy, but to me, they were just words. But I played on those words... used those people who believed in me... and over a short period of time, I accumulated a great deal of wealth. I had my first billion by age 23, and that is the year I invented *LifeSim™*. I used a half-billion of my own money... and several billion of others as funding to create the greatest game in the world. Now, I had been working on several versions of the game since I was fifteen, but once I got the financial backing I needed, I went into high gear... and within a year the *Sim Game* was ready to test. We sent lots of people through the *STR* portal... and they all came back safely."

"Sorry, first question... what is *STR* portal?"

"Space-time reference'. Somehow, and I was never exactly sure how, I was able to create the game across various space and time-lines. Meaning, the game could be set 21st century New York City, 20th century Egypt, 23rd century Barcelona, or even 19th century London... which, BTW, was where I was right before I arrived here."

I stop take a breath. "Do you need to go throw up... or anything?" I ask.

"Not yet... but I've decided to take notes, and maybe turn this into a really great science fiction novel."

"Be my guest... okay, but now is where it gets complicated..."

"Excuse me... NOW is where it gets complicated?"

"Okay, poor choice of words. Now it where it gets really... really complicated."

"Better."

"Not sure you are taking this discussion serious?"

"We'll see... please continue."

"What I did... with the help of others, was create this extremely complex algorithm. It takes elements from location... time... real events... made up scenarios, and throws them all together in a big pile, which I called a *Sim*. Much of the data was extracted directed from the Web... internet, as they still called it in my day. What I was trying to achieve was what I called... the universal randomness of life. The purpose was for folks to take an adventure... in one of the many *Sim* worlds we created, which they were able to pre-select... and once they returned... they would want to take another... and another. The problem is, most folks... adventures, gamers... are easily bored... they take the same adventure twice and they are done. My main objective was to provide endless variables... so each time you entered the game... things would be different... and never the same."

"Well, unfortunately... I succeeded. After less than a year of testing, my partners wanted to implement the game, and we created a small sales force... who were able to sell a million copies of version 1.0 of the game... before we even released it. Well, based on the complexity of the game... I demanded more testing... and my primary partner balked. He let me know he had hundreds of millions invested... and he needed to recoup those funds... now."

I stop and take a sip of wine, which Jasmine has just refreshed, "Well, being the inventor and major stakeholder, I balked, and we had a serious argument. In the end, he told me... if you want further testing... then you go... test to your heart's content... and then return... so we can open the damn game. But, of course he did not call it the damn-game but rather the *G--damned* game. That royally pissed me off."

"I was not interested in doing that, and declined his offer, but unfortunately, when you have stockholders and stakeholders, you are not always in charge. In the end... 47 % of the investors wanted the game to go live. At that point, our presales were close to a billion."

"So, why were you hesitating... if everyone felt the game was ready to go?"

"Yes, well that is certainly the question of the day. And the short answer is… I do not know. Something about the game always disturbed me… it was like, somehow… it had a mind of its own. Yes, there were rules… but those rules seem to 'bend' much too easily… the environment would… let's call it evolve, for lack of a better term. Nothing major, at first… just little stuff. For example, one of the Sim characters… would act out of character. I would go back and check the programming… but it was always accurate. At one point I ran a compare between the base program and the current program… and identified over 5000 variances. Anyway, I won't bore you with the technical stuff. In the end, I agreed to do a final two week beta test, and if that passed my inspection… I further agreed to let the game go public."

"So is that when to entered the Sim Game… and never returned?" Jasmine asks, I can see she is now taking this very serious.

"Yes. I entered in Sim, spent two week documenting my experience… I found a few bugs… and a couple of anomalies that disturbed me."

"Enough to prevent the game from going into production?" Jasmine asks.

"Yes, unfortunately I did. Some of the characters and base scenarios were changed, from my original programming… and I needed to find out why… before releasing the game to the public."

"And then what happened?" Jasmine asks.

"Well, I send my report in right before my scheduled returned, went to the assigned return portal… but it was not there. I've been looking for an exit door ever since."

"And what is an exit door?" Jasmine asks.

"Each Sim I created has at least one Exit Door… designed to facilitate in-game maintenance."

"So why did you not use one of those doors to extract yourself from the game."

"Well, first, I did not take the ED location program with me… since I already had my assigned exit point. And, second…

I've been unable to find any exit door... in any of the *Sims* I visited in the last eleven years."

"Okay, I'm beginning to get a clearer picture of the situation..."

"And yet... you are still here," I reply.

"Only because my legs are unable or unwilling to move... not sure which. But I do have one more question. Do you think your trip to beta test the *Sim* was sabotaged?"

"Now that is the best question of all, and believe it or not... I never considered that possibility until I got here, and read my *obituary*."

"Now... I think it's time to run... flee for my life... my sanity... both." Jasmine states... but she remains seated. I wait... giving her every opportunity to save herself before it is too late.

"And now?" she asks.

"And now, what?" I respond.

"And now... do you believe your return was sabotaged."

"Yes, unfortunately, after reading my obituary, I believe my partner somehow prevented me from exiting the game... and later declared me dead... and inherited my two plus billion credit estate."

"Oh... two plus billion credit estate... now that explains the unlimited credit *Keycard*."

"Not really. Since my partner inherited my estate in 2058... I am certain he would have transferred all of my assets and funds to his own account... and yet, here I am still spending credits like there is no tomorrow."

"Okay, I now have enough for a full trilogy... so we can stop, for now."

"Full trilogy?" I question.

"You remember that science fiction novel I'll be writing based on the story you've just narrated."

"Do people even read Sci-Fi novels in 2350?"

"People will always read Sci-Fi novels... folks are always interested in what the future holds... may hold... could hold in some alternate universe... nothing has really changed. When folks stop reading SF novels… then that means their curiosity has stopped… and the world will really be in deep shit."

Pay It Forward

"So where to from here?" I ask, uncertain if Jasmine will want to continue having a relationship with a certified psychopath.

"I move in, of course… unless you object," she responds.

"No that would be great… but."

"Damn I just hate buts… not your specific butt, however."

"No, what I mean is that I have not told you the entire story. So let me make this part quick. While I am not longer convinced I am in one of my created *Sims*, I still fear that. And if I am in my *Sim*… then soon I will *Reset*… and one moment… I will be gone. Can you handle that?"

"No… and if you ever do that to me… I will hunt you down… through space and time if necessary… and you will be sorry!" Jasmine responds.

"Okay, then in order for me to get beyond my belief that we remain in a *Sim*… I need you to convince me that this environment… place… City… is real."

"Well, first, I'm insulted… could a *Sim* ever make love to you as good as I did?"

"I refuse to answer on the grounds that it may tend to get me slapped in the face… and possibly disfigured. Honestly, Jasmine, we designed the *Sims* to look, feel, act, and even taste like humans. Emotionally… they have the full range… hard to tell them from humans… except, of course…"

"Ah, I believe I may like the 'of course'."

"What got me thinking this could be a real world was the fact that you did not work a full 24/7 shift…"

"Wow, you really were slave drivers… did the *Sims* not even get a day off… to refresh their circuits… or something like that."

"No, and the reason why is simple. We did not create an unlimited number of *Sim* humans. Since most folks would be in the game for two or three days… a week at the most, then we did not need shifts. A *Sim* bartender, for example, would work 24/7. Now, over time they may evolve… and may even be replaced… but that is based on a feedback loop algorithm I developed which has to do with customer satisfaction…"

"Never mind the details, I understand you techie guys can go on forever, but I believe I understand the gist of it. So, I need to prove I'm human… okay… tell me one thing a *Sim* would never do in public… even an evolved *Sim*?

"No. let's not go there. I would not want to create an embarrassing scene… if this is actually a real environment.

"If you want to have sex in public… I can do that… would a *Sim*?

"Yes."

"Damn… there went my Ace in the hole."

"Now that's funny… and *Sims* are *not* often funny. Since humor is very subjective… we keep the humor to a minimum… so as not to offend."

"Would a *Sim* ever tell you that you can be, at times… the most obstinate person in the universe?"

"No, a *Sim* would never insult a human."

"And neither would I."

"Okay, let's work on that… but if you are able to convince me this is a real world… and not a *Sim*… then I have an even larger issue to overcome."

"What?"

"No, 'How'… how could I have exited the *Sim*, and then entered the real-world … and in 2350?"

"No… I meant… never mind… we will work on that… whenever you are convinced. But, for now… did you notice that I did not leave, running and screaming from your hotel room, when you told me your story?"

"Yes, I did, but I assumed it was the profit motive that kept you here… you see a big paycheck when you actually write that Sci-Fi novel…"

"Oh I already have enough to write that novel... I don't need anything else from you on that. But that does bring up a problem."

"Which is?"

"How can I convince you I am not after your money? I already know you are super-rich... I have no idea how rich and do not want to know."

"You've already proven that to me... so never bring it up again. If I have unlimited funds, for whatever reason... then so do you. Yes, please move in today... and if I am still here in another month... then let's buy the largest home, with the best view... in all of *CloudCity*."

"Hum... not as good as I had hoped... but will probably do... in the short term," Jasmine responses, and then breaks into a small, but meaningful smile.

"Okay, well a ring... of course..."

"Not interested... rings are so 21st century..."

"What then?"

"I refuse to reveal all of my secrets this early in the game."

...

"Okay, so where do we start with me convincing you that *CloudCity* is real and not a Sim?"

"I have a few prelim questions I could ask?"

"Shoot!"

"Do you have monsters that roam the streets at night after dark, or on a full moon?"

"Other than you... No."

"Uh, a 'Yes' or 'No' will suffice."

"That is no fun. Can I get more wine to see me through this?"

"No. Next question... have you ever detected any repeating patterns, either in the way the city is laid out, designed, built or even operates?'

"If I understand your question correctly... then no. Each section of *Cloud City* is entirely different. It was originally decided, back in 2208, when they first conceived of floating a city… or cities above the surface of the earth, that all of the cities would be different… no common pattern or design, and that within each city, there would be both architectural and cultural diversity. The goal was full integration of all *Sky Cities*. There is no *Sky City* where just the Irish live, or Russians, or Chinese… or Japanese. Everyone lives anywhere they want… within financial and practical reason."

"Thanks for the simple 'Yes' or 'No'."

"You're welcome. You done?"

"You wish. Next question…"

"If I can't have a glass of wine, then how about a scotch?"

"Later… next question, Are there any large castles close by, either up here in Cloud City or down on the surface of the planet?"

"No… no castles, no witches, warlocks… or even vampire bats… unfortunately, they all died out sometime in the last 21st century."

"Your brevity of response is most appreciated."

"I'm accommodating,"

"Yes, you are. How about games… are there an excessive number of gaming places in town… that require extra payment… you know… gambling houses, video games with in-app purchases…"

"Yes… I know… If you will stop talking for a sec… I will answer your question… No."

"No, what?"

"Damn, you really are the most frustrating human on the planet!"

"Last question… am I the *only* human on the planet?"

"Is that a trick question?"

"Yes."

"I'm done… scotch or wine for you?" Jasmine asks as she breaks for the kitchen.

"Wine is good… and what took you so long to ask… you are such a bad host." Jasmine returns with the wine and a small plate of food snacks.

"You never did answer my question about the video games, gambling, and arcades."

"Okay, yes, gambling is allowed but only if you have a valid 'gaming' license, and yes, there are video arcades and gaming-houses on *Cloud City*... and all *Sky Cities*... BUT... none of them allow in-app purchases. That little trick was outlawed way back in... well, not sure when... but that was outlawed. It took advantage of the weak of mind, the excessive/compulsive, and the bad gambler... anything else before we drink our wine... and end this interrogation."

"No... that's it... and I believe I have my answer. This... by all accounts... is a real world, and not a *Sim*," I state, rather proud of my powers of reasoning and deduction.

"Oh thank you so much for certifying us as real... will we get a Certificate to hang on the wall?"

"No, that is an in-app purchase and will cost you an extra ten credits."

"Figures."

Reality Based... Reality

Jasmine moves in the very next day, but also decides to keep her job at the bar, "I really enjoy bartending, and talking to folks... any objection?"

"Absolutely not... as long as I get a discount on drinks?"

"Are you serious... you pay list price for those 25 YO scotches... actually... slightly above list... and I expect to get the same size tips as before... no discount... understood?"

"Yes, understood."

"Good. I have a few things I'll need to move in... how do we handle that?"

"Oh, let's wait a month... don't give up your apartment until we find a home... and then move all of your stuff into the home."

"Okay, I can do that."

"Now, I can pick up the rent until then..."

"Not necessary... I do not intend to be a 'kept' woman."

...

I spend much of the next few weeks observing... fact checking... analyzing. I need to determine for sure that this 'reality' is not a *Sim*... before I buy a home, and settle down for the rest of my life. Most importantly, I have not forgotten about Joyce... or Brenda... or even Kathy. They are in my thoughts... and my prayers. But for now... I need to live in the moment. *If... ever...* then I will revisit the situation.

Pat calls a few times, checking up on me. I let her know... I've met someone. She seems disappointed... but such is life. I spend a lot of my daytime hours (mostly when Jasmine is at work) walking the streets of the City... trying to figure everything out. So far... everything appears to be real... and I am growing more hopeful each day. But... also, each day I am thinking about Brenda, Joyce, and Kathy. I can't seem to let them go. I am responsible for their fate, and even though I've moved on... I must find some way to save them. Not sure we could all fit in 2350... but I need to resolve their individual timelines and rectify their current unacceptable situation. Now, even though Brenda is deceased... does not cause me to give up hope on her. If I am able to return to the past... the Sim past... then maybe I can return early enough to save Brenda from Jack. If I could get me hands on Jack... for just five minutes... things would definitely be different.

Now I Am Really Fucked!

"So are you happy now?" Jasmine asks.

"Well, I am extremely happy to know you are real... and also delighted that I ended up back in a reality-based world... but I still need to find my way back... I have lots of unfinished business to attend to in the past... and don't believe I can ever be truly happy until the problems of my past have been... successfully resolved."

"Oh, Jim... I am sorry to hear that. Can't you just be happy living in the present... or the *Now* as we call it?"

"I am happy... you make me happy... but there is still more story to be told... and once you understand it all... you will appreciate why I have to find my way back."

"If you go back, then I will never see you again... and honestly, Jim... I love you... warts and all."

"What warts?" I ask, total surprised by that comment.

"We don't have that much time before... well... the end of the world."

I decide that now would be a good time to change the subject... "Where shall we go tonight? The sky is, literally, the limit." I am, again, so proud of myself.

"Let's stay at the hotel... order room service... or we could go up to the bar... no, guess I'm a bit tired of that place... same ole same ole."

"Which is why I suggested we go out... figured you were tired of everything this hotel had to offer."

"No... I am not tired of you... everything else, is just secondary."

...

It is 10AM before we awake, and unfortunately, Jasmine has to work the 11AM to 6PM shift. "But what will I do without you?" I ask, as she dresses to leave for work.

"I suggest you brush up on recent world history... since 2050... that may provide the answers to some of your questions. Jim... I understand you need answers, and will do everything I can to help you find them. But, I have a request."

"Okay, I'm listening."

"If you do decide to go back to the past... and you find a way to do so, then please... take me with you. If somehow we get lost in the past, then at least we will be together."

Wow... that was unexpected. "I will consider that... and don't worry; I will do nothing without discussing it with you first."

"Thanks... I need to go... see you at six."

"Can I come up and visit you?"

"Not today... I expect to be slammed all day."

...

Well, Jasmine told me *what* to do... but not *how* to do it. I need to research, but how should I go about that... ah... public library, history and art museums... I can handle that.

I start with the public library. I spot a bank of view terminals lined up along the side wall. Several are unoccupied, so I head toward one of them. As I take a seat at one of the inactive one, the screen displays, "Welcome Dr. Caldwell... what can we do for you today?"

I type "Research past between 2050 and present." I assume it read my *Keycard,* and reacted accordingly.

"Please narrow search... history of what? I have a selection index if you prefer." I start with the index, and begin my research. The computers in 2350 are extremely intuitive, every time I make a selection, everything on the screen changes. There are often between six and ten sub-panels open at any one time, each conveying different information. If I want that specific information, then I press that panel and it opens to become the primary. It takes me less than 30 minutes to become proficient… and I am quickly scanning through data… taking links, and retaining data in a personal-holding area.

Two hours later, I'm done. Well, it is all I can handle. It was intensive, and my fingers and eyes are fatigued. My final question is, "How do I retrieve the data I've stored?"

"Any time you log into any terminal, your stored data is available… simply look for the icon with your photo… and press it. I had not seen that before, but look at the screen and in the upper right hand corner is my face… so I press it, and it opens all of the data I've accumulated to date. I look for sharing options… and see them at the bottom of the screen. I look for *SmartComm*… nothing. But I do locate *P*Comm. I press and the screen selections roll up. I spot 'Download data to *P*Comm'. I press that button. The alarm beeps on my *SmartComm* and a message displays on screen, "Data downloaded and correlated. Remote *OpSys* out of date and no longer supported. Base data is stored… but the relationships remain unresolved."

I leave the library with renewed hope. I went through Earth's history from 2050 to 2350, and much has changed, not only in the technology areas, but in all areas of life. Part of our solution to conquer global warming, which was at critical mass back in 2050, was to create self-sufficient and 100% recyclable environments in the sky… *SkyCities*. Others included the invention of *Instantaneous Mass Transport* (IMT), virtually eliminating all automobile and flight-vehicle production within twenty years. "Wish I had invented that." I grin to myself as I continue to remember the history I read.

It took over a hundred years (2080-2203) before the first *SkyCity* was floated above the Earth. But, once they started floating away from the Earth… they never stopped. There are, at present, almost two hundred cities floating above planet Earth. *CloudCity* was neither the first nor is it the largest. There are, believe it or not, still almost a billion folks living on the surface. It seems that once the big cities took flight… the pollution index started going down… and after the first hundred cities were floating above the surface, the surface temperature of the Earth actual began to decline. Another hundred cities were floated, and at that point, many of the more rural residents decided to stay. The last *SkyCity* was launched almost fifty years ago… and no more are currently planned.

Well, if I had any remaining doubts, they are gone. No one would create such an elaborate *Sim*… yes, we had web portals in our Sims, but actually, they were linked to the real-web… we did not have the kind of funds required to fabricate a *Sim* history… so we never bothered.

I return to the hotel… enlightened. Already, ideas are forming in my head, just based on what I read, and stored in my personal file. It is still two hours before Jasmine is off duty, so I head to the lobby-level bar, pull up a scotch and have a seat (or is it pull up a seat and have a scotch… not sure it matters).

I am consuming my second scotch and reviewing the data downloaded to my *SmartComm*, when I first notice someone has taken the seat at the bar next to me. I glance over, it's a cute female… maybe 22… and she smiles, "Mind if I sit here… the bar is rather crowded."

I look around the bar… there are only seven other guests in the entire bar area at the moment, "Sure… no problem." I return to my research.

It is not long before I feel a hand on my leg and moving toward my crotch. "Excuse me, miss… while I appreciate the attention, I have already found the love of my life, so if you would please discontinue your approach to my vital parts… I would greatly appreciate that… and have a good day." She moves away quickly, and I return to my research. 2350 is, after all, not so different than 2050.

…

I am back in the hotel room when Jasmine arrives, "How was your shift?"

"Boring, mad, frustrating… remind me again why I am doing this?"

"You wanted the human interaction… I believe it was something like that."

"Yea, well, it's overrated. I was hit on twice today… and one guy actually put his hand on my crotch."

"And what did you do?" I inquire.

"Well, I slapped the shit out of him… what do you think?"

"Good for you."

"And your day?"

"Research went wonderful. I downloaded a ton of data that should help us return to the past."

"So, I can go with you?"

"Of course… if I am able to go back in time… then we will go together, because, as you said before… life without you is life not worth living."

"I wish I had said that, but didn't," she replies. "So what did you do after your research ended?"

"Oh, I came back here, went to the lobby bar, had a couple of scotches, and then came home."

"Anything you want to discuss regarding your experience at the lobby bar?"

"Other than some cute girl trying to grab my crotch… no."

"I saw that… we have personal proximity alerts, and you came up on my screen. I should not have looked… but I couldn't help myself… I'm sorry."

"No problem… I am interested in no one, but you."

Current Goals... and Future Aspirations

"Okay, I'm ready to discuss the rest of your past. I realize I was not the first... the only love in your life... so tell me about the others, especially the ones you want to go back into the *Sim* past and save."

"Well, believe it or not, there have not been all that many."

"I can believe that."

"That was not a question... I had one love before I left 2050... but she is long gone so I will not even discuss her. Let's start with Kathy."

"And were you and Kathy lovers?" Jasmine asks.

"No, basically... we hated each other... and in this case, opposites did not attracted... they repelled, big time."

"So why do you want to save her?"

"Because she became trapped in the *Sim*... and somehow I caused that... not sure it matters how... but I have an obligation to get her out of there and back to her home."

"What do you want to tell me about Kathy?"

"Not much, I was able to set her up in the best hotel suite in town... and hopefully she is still there... living well... waiting to be rescued."

"And the rest?"

"Let's discuss Joyce... I was in love with her, and we were torn apart by my *Reset* from the 1890's London *STR*." I am going to tell the truth... hold nothing back.

"Did you love her more than me?" Jasmine asks.

"I loved her... a lot. I'm not sure I can quantify love... while I was with her, I loved no one but her, and was depressed when I *Reset* and lost her."

"And what about Brenda… did you love her, too?"

"No, we had just met, but she was Joyce's friend. That was the tragedy."

"What happened?"

"I will keep this short and not get into details… have you ever heard of Jack the Ripper?"

"No, I don't think so… sound like a bad guy, and we've purged most of our evil villains from our history… was just not enough room to store everything… so something had to go."

"Well, back in 1890 London, Jack was a real character. Somehow in my 1890 London *Sim*… he showed up… and started killing females… but only real females… not Sims."

"I am not following, but then I don't follow at lot of what you tell me… please proceed."

"Anyway, right before I *Reset* from 1890 London, Joyce and I were coming back from dinner and a play… and we got back to the hotel room… and found Brenda… torn to pieces… body parts and blood scattered all around the room… it was horrible… I can still see Joyce bent over her torso… throwing up…"

"So, you want to go back and save Brenda… and do what with Joyce?"

"That is a fair question… and I'm not sure. I did love her… and I must save Brenda… everything else is… in flux."

"Okay, fair enough… anything else you need to tell me before I get totally depressed and head for bed?"

"Only that I love you… have never loved anyone more than you… and need your help getting back… and fixing this mess I created."

"Okay, you know I'll help… and I am especially looking forward to meeting this Joyce person."

"No violence… she's been through a lot."

"I promise… I will not throw the first punch, but other than that… all bets are off."

"Fair enough."

"So how do we go about getting back to the past… and the *Sim* past?'

"Now, that, Jasmine is the question of the century."

Plan of Action... Against All Odds

We decide to relax, and move away from this entire conversation. We make love, but the intensity is not there. There is hesitation, on both our parts. Yes, I loved Joyce... and yes I love Jasmine. I hate that we had to have that conversation, because it certainly fucked up our good time.

We become a bit distant with each other. Since our conversation, I seem to be lost in to past.... I love Jasmine as much as ever... but remember that I loved Joyce... and will, most likely, always love Joyce. Jasmine decides she needs to get out, and be alone for a while. I understand. This is a heavy load to bear. I wish I could just forget my past... and live in the present as Jasmine recommends... but that is not going to happen. I will go back. I will rectify the wrongs of the past... and then, if any part of me remains, I will return to live my life with Jasmine.

I decide to leave the hotel, as well, and I wonder the streets... looking for what? I have everything I've been looking for... right here and right now. What else could I possibly want? I have never been happier, and I realize, happiness is not a guarantee... it is a privilege, and when you finally achieve happiness... do not look it in the mouth or in the eye, just embrace it and go with it... because... it may never come again.

I return to the hotel suite several hours later... and have made my decision. I will stay here... live in the *Now*... and fulfill my destiny with Jasmine.

As I enter the suite, I spot Jasmine, sitting on the couch, drinking a glass of wine. I walk directly to her, "I've changed my mind... you are the love of my life... I will stay here with you... forever... until I die. Nothing else matters."

"Thank you, Jim… I appreciate that… BUT… that is not what is going to happen. I too have been thinking, and I have come to this conclusion… if you don't go back, confront and deal with your past… then it will always be there to haunt us… and we will never be truly happy. We must go back… we must save your friends… and then we can move forward… whatever that means."

Part 3
Rectifying Past Mistakes

Planning for the Past

I decide to share the information I'm obtained, and is now stored in my *SmartComm*. Jasmine uploads all of the data to her *P*Comm, which is linked to her private network, and it displays on her visual wall.

"Okay so what are we looking for, Jim?" Jasmine asks, once we see the data scrolling through the display.

"We need to correlate the reference points in my *SmartComm* with the data I have downloaded. I am certain I'm downloaded a few terabytes, and have sufficient data to triangulate where we need to get to."

"Well, that makes no sense. How will we use this data, to get to the past? I have no time portal we can use to get us from here to there."

"Hang in there… we are just getting started. I believe we have the technology to do this… but we need to break it down… step by step.

We spend the better part of the next week, analyzing the data… linking the various attributes. I use the same process I employed to create the original *Sim...* intelligence, ingenuity, inspiration, and lots of perspiration.

…

We are six days into the process, and we do not seem to be any closer to the answer. I look as Jasmine, "Anytime you want to give up, let me know… I am committed to YOU… I love you and the rest of it… well… we tried but failed."

"I will not give up… let's try reversing the process. Instead of making the data from this space-time reference as primary…

let's switch off and make the data from your past the primary driver."

"Excellent idea… I had not thought of that." And as simple as that idea sounded… it begins to work. The data begins to link… forming a pattern and then some semblance of a plan. The result of the data correlation is a map… a map to the past. But, unfortunately that still does not get to the actual past, and only becomes useful once we actually arrive in the past.

Unfortunately, back in 2048, I had a huge mainframe computer to work with… and used those powerful facilities to build the Sims, and integrate the humans into those Sims, "Got it!" I state, "Well, half of it at least."

"Okay, let's talk," Jasmine discontinues her research, and looks directly at me.

"We will go back to 2048, the real *STR*, and I will gain access to my mainframe, and we will go into the *Sims* as I designed them… through the entrance portal."

"But, wouldn't that cause the same issues as before… we would both be trapped in time and *Sim*… so where is the advantage?"

"Not if I've drawn the correct conclusions from my analysis and from my gut feelings. I now believe I was set up to fail. When I failed to agree to open the gates to hell without further testing, I now believe my partner and… best friend, somehow sabotaged the game so once I got inside… I would never be able to get out."

"Is that possible?"

"All things are possible, Jasmine, given enough motive. And my old partner had that motive… two billion credits worth of motive."

"How did he accomplish it?"

"Not sure that matters. Our challenge is to go back to the past… to before Francis Jamison made whatever changes he made… then go into the *Sims*, and return those folks to their rightful *STR*."

"Okay, that makes sense… assuming you are correct in your assumptions of a sabotage."

"Yes, assuming that."

"So, now comes the easy part... how do we get to the past?" Jasmine asks, as if pondering that impossible scenario.

"I believe I already have that one solved. I was able to get here to the future, correct... so all I need to do is reverse the process. Remember, my *SmartComm* captures all data in real-time, and stores that data. Much of that has already been correlated into recent planet history and considering current advancements in technology. All I have to do is reverse the..."

"Wait... I see where you are going, but that won't work." Jasmine interrupts.

"And why not?" I counter.

"Because you arrived from a Sim... inside the game and not from real-space... so, yes, you would go back in time right where you left it.... Standing in that bedroom looking at parts of Brenda and watching Joyce throw up."

"Hum... seems you have a point worth considering," I suggest.

"Well, thanks for that... I guess."

...

We decide to stop, take a break, and think in background mode for a while. Lunch is served, al la... the cart. We eat, but skip the wine... we will need all of our brain cells to successfully navigate through this problem.

"Jasmine, as much as I appreciate your decision to continue working at the bar... I would suggest that now is the time to resign... we have, possibly weeks or even months of work ahead of us before we are able to travel back in time... correct these... issues, and return. And when we return... I am not certain this timeline will be exactly the same as it was when we left."

"Not the same... what do you mean?"

"We will, most likely make changes in the past, and those changes will have a ripple effect... ramifications... time waves... that will bubble up into the future. In theory, even small changes made in the past... could dramatically change the future… so we need to carefully consider everything we do, while in the past."

"So, I might end up being my mother's Grandma, or my sister's brother?" Jasmine, replies, and I can now see how serious she is NOT taking this precaution.

"Something like that… but as long as you remain a female… I will still love you."

"Are you a same-sex bigot?"

"No, I just like your equipment so much better… it fits…"

"Got it. So why will we make changes at all?"

"Well, in the current future, I never came back from the *Sim*, and neither did Joyce, Brenda, Kathy or the other 'girls' in her group. And, my partner became a rich man… at my personal expense."

"So, all of that would be changed… I get that, but is that significant… why will that cause a ripple effect in time?" she asks.

"Because I plan to kill my partner… that is why!"

Mitigating Past Mistakes

"You can't be serious, Jim. I know you... and you are not a murderer."

"No, I am not, but I do believe in revenge... and I want to watch as Jack the Ripper cuts my ex-partner into little pieces."

"What does that mean?"

"My plan is to retrieve all of the people... he marooned in the past... I believe he is responsible for all of it... he was certainly bright enough... then I'm going to send him back to take Brenda's place... just as Jack begins cutting on Brenda... oops.. the ole switch-a-roo... out dissolves Brenda and in dissolves Francis. So you see, I won't actually kill him... he will be killed by his on greed... now that is revenge."

"Not sure I love you anymore, Jim... that is cruel and unusual punishment."

"Had you seen the piece parts of one of your good friends scattered all over the room... floor, walls, even the ceiling, I believe you would feel differently."

"Yes, maybe, but I didn't witness that monstrous act... and I strongly advise you not to live your life seeking revenge... it is negative... and serves no purpose. Make sure he pays for his crimes... but DO NOT KILL HIM!"

"I can't make that promise."

"I believe, when the time comes... you can... but we will leave this right here for now... I do love you, but cannot and will not live with a murderer... regardless of the reason."

"Okay... got it!"

...

Maybe we should have drank some wine, after all, because by the end of that discussion, I am more agitated than ever... and so is Jasmine. I decide it is my time to make things right, "I'm sorry... I am not a violent person, please understand that... but what I saw... will haunt me for the rest of my life. And to see the woman I love, on her knees throwing up over her best friend's torso... how can I ever accept that."

"But, Jim... that is the point, we do not have to accept it... we can go back and change it... so it never happened."

"Jasmine, you are... possibly... the wisest person I've even met."

"Possibly?"

...

Jasmine decides to quit her job, after all, and gives the standard one week notice. She is, of course, given the worse shifts possible for her last week, but she expected that, and if she can handle it, then so can I.

I spend the week working on a process to reverse the time travel event that brought me here, but instead of returning to the point of the Sim that I left, I am substituting all of the time attributes of my first successful *Sim* test, in October 2048. This was months before my 'partner' became involved in the project... we were friends, and we discussed the project all the time, over drinks and such, but, if memory serves, it was not until January of 2049, that he finally came on board... offering a hundred-million credits as his 'buy in'.

By Friday, I believe I have at least a working prototype of a crude time machine. But, how to test it...? And in order to do this, I must have access to a mainframe... if such a thing even exits in 2350.

Jasmine does not arrive home until after 2AM... she is beat... but only one more day to go. I am still working on my prototype... so we kiss, and she heads to bed. There will be no sex tonight... and I end up working through it. I finally get to bed at 6AM, and by ten Jasmine is up and getting ready for her last day. "I work from 11AM to 6PM... let's go somewhere special tonight… to celebrate the end of my career as a Bartender at the most famous Bar in all of *CloudCity*."

"You got it… wherever you want to go… I will take you there."

"Thanks Jim."

I search the web looking for 'computer service leases… short term.' I find very little, and decide this will have to wait until Jasmine is back, full time, on the project. I spend the day, once again walking the town. It is another pleasant day in *CloudCity*. The temp is 70 degrees, and it is partly cloudy… with a small possibility of rain. I am really loving this city… and fully believe that, once this sorry affair is over, Jasmine and I will settle here, for the rest of our lives.

Time Heals All Wounds

We restart our project on Monday. Jasmine has a few ideas regarding acquiring some short-term mainframe computer power. Everything has gone local networking, but once you log into the network… there is power to spare. I contact the 'host' and sign up for six months of 'unlimited capacity'.

By Wednesday, we are linked in, and I download all of my correlated data into my 'private work space'. We run several *Sims*, and they all work… as *Sims* almost always do. "Well, I need to actually test the program… and for that… you are NOT invited to attend. Assuming I am back and in one piece… hopefully in a few seconds, then we can plan our trip to the past… and we will then be ready to go."

"Do you believe this will work?"

"Yes, I do. This was no more difficult than creating the *Sim Game*… and all of that data was stored in the *SmartComm*… all 1600 TB.

"Okay, but I must admit… I am a bit… apprehensive," Jasmine states, as she takes hold of my hand.

"It will be alright… but if for some reason I do not make it back… then please know that I love you… more than anything in this world."

"How will you do it… didn't you have, like a teleporter or something before?"

"Yes, that initiated the process, but once I was inside the Sim, then the information came from my *SmartComm*… and it's all stored right here, but we need the power of the mainframe to make it all work. Since I have a direct link from the mainframe to my *SmartComm*… everything should be fine."

"Okay… so quickly, tell me again the exact plan for this final test."

"Sure, I will head back in time to October 2048, and arrive inside my lab. This was immediately before I entered the *Sim* for the actual first real test… which worked perfectly… BTW. I should have a couple of minutes alone. All I want to do is verify I have returned to the point I am seeking, and then I will come back here… immediately."

"Okay… I love you."

I retrieve my *SmartComm,* 'EXE' the program, and then press 'GO'.

...

I am in my lab… everything looks the same. I walk over and touch the Portal… it is real. I turn to head back to my point of origin… and there I am standing looking at… myself. "What the fuck… what is going on? Cloning has been outlawed for a hundred years… and I would have known… what is this?"

I realize this is bad news… and anything I do now may cause a shift in the timeline… and ripple forward… causing… who knows what."

"Hi, Jim… I'm just your dream… telling you, your test will be successful… do not worry… and do not change a thing." I have the *SmartComm* in my hand, and quickly press RETURN… and I am back with Jasmine.

"Did it not work? I saw you dissolve out of existence, but then immediately back in… what happened?"

"It worked… but, unfortunately, my timing was slightly off and I met myself from the past… never a good thing."

"Shit, what happened?"

"Well, I told him, it, me… it was a dream… and that everything would be fine… and then I returned…"

"Sounds like a smart move. Good choice."

"Yea… and I could really use a drink about now."

"Let's go out… drinks… dinner… maybe a show… the whole thing… we need to celebrate. You, my friend, are the first person in history… to travel through time." Jasmine states, all proud.

"No I am the second."

"Who was the first?"

"That was me… too."

"Ass-hole!"

"Yep, and proud of it."

Returning to the Past

"Okay, time to go. Pack light... I don't believe we have room for any overnight bags," I state. Jasmine just looks at me, slowly shaking her head. "Okay, just to review, once we are back in 2048, I will program the Game-Sim Computer for each of the destinations... and one at a time, we will retrieve our 'guests' and return them to the present... reality. We will start with Kathy, and then Joyce, Brenda... and hopefully the other 'girls' trapped in 1890."

"Yea, I am really looking forward to meeting Joyce... but promise to be on my best behavior..." Jasmine interjects.

"Then, once those tasks have been accomplished, we will return to 2048. You will then head back to 2350... and I will take care of my old ex-partner."

"Remember... no killing," Jasmine states.

"Remember... no promises," I respond.

...

We decide to head back five minutes earlier than my test trip... I do not want to meet myself again... that was... uncanny... uncomfortable... and unpleasant (and probably very unwise).

"Are you ready to visit the past?" I ask, as I take hold of Jasmine's hand.

"No, I believe I've changed my mind... let me stay here... prepare dinner..."

"No way... we are a team... let's go. She smiles, nods, and I press the 'GO' Button... and we are back in my lab at *FgU*,

October 2048. I quickly look around... and do not see me... that maybe a good omen.

I head to the master console, plug in my *SmartComm*, and press 'Download Pre-selected Data'. The portal light turns green, I retake Jasmine's hand and we enter the portal.

We arrive right outside the *Imperial Hotel*, as programmed. I can only hope that Kathy still lives here. I decided to give it a couple of months between the time I left and when I return. That will make it easier to explain my absence. If this does not work, I can preprogram for an earlier return... one step at a time.

I walk into the hotel, and there is the same desk clerk, although I have forgotten his name, "Welcome back Mr. Caldwell... we've missed you. If you are looking for Kathy, I believe she is out at the moment, but do expect her back by six. Head over to the bar, have a couple of drinks and once she returns, I'll let her know you are here. I am certain she will be pleased to see you.

I nod, do not introduce Jasmine, and we head to the bar. "Ashamed to introduce me?" she asks.

"There is no need to introduce you to all of the *Sims* we meet... for obvious reasons." I reply.

"Are you a *Sims* bigot, as well?" Jasmine asks, but she smiles, giving herself away.

We head into the bar, and there is Joe... tending bar, "Mr. Caldwell... welcome back... scotch, sir?"

"Yes, Joe, please."

"And for the lady?" Joe inquires.

"The same, please, Joe," Jasmine responds.

We take a seat at the bar, and Joe returns shortly with our drinks. I check my *SmartComm*... it is 5:15PM local time, so we have a while. We sip our drinks and try to relax. It is about 6:05 when I hear a scream in the lobby. Jasmine and I both look toward the lobby and here comes Kathy... running toward me screaming, "Oh my God... oh my God... you came back." I stand and she runs into my arms… we hug but do not kiss. "Welcome back to *Sims Palace*!" she states.

"Glad to be back, and this is the love of my life, Jasmine. Jasmine this is Kathy… can we go somewhere and talk?" I ask.

"Nice to meet you, Jasmine… let's talk right here… I'm free, for a while anyway."

Kathy orders wine, and we move to a private table. Once Kathy's drink arrives, we relax and Kathy begins, "It is so good to see you… what's it been, three months? Believe it or not… I've really missed you…. But, why are you back?"

"I told you I'd come back for you… and that is exactly what I'm doing. Anytime you are ready… we can get out of this dammed Sim… and get you back home."

"So, you did find a way out… good for you, I never doubted that for a moment." Kathy looks at Jasmine, "Did Jim tell you about our love-hate relationship?"

"He told me all about the hate part… but I don't remember him mentioning any 'love' part."

"That's because there wasn't one! We basically disliked each other from the moment we met… but in the end, Jim saved my life… and I am forever grateful," Kathy smiles, and looks back at me.

"Let's have dinner together… and then later, you can meet Gail… the love of *my* life," Kathy adds.

"You found someone here…. Good, so you have not been alone!"

"For the first few weeks… yes… but hey, you set me up so nice that it was just a matter of time… and I met Gail, and well… things have been wonderful ever since."

"I hate to ask, but is Gail a human or a *Sim*?" I ask.

"Does it matter… love is love."

"But, if Gail is a Sim, then we cannot take her with us when we leave…"

"Leave… why would we leave?"

"Well, I thought that was obvious… you are trapped inside a Sim game, and I have come back, as promised, to rescue you."

"Well, I guess that is a problem… because… honestly, I don't want to be rescued. I have it all. A swanky Penthouse apartment, all the money in the world, and the girl I love… what else could I possibly want?" Kathy asks, now looking somewhat puzzled.

Well, I am stumped, so Jasmine takes over the conversation, while I take a rather large sip of scotch.

"So, are you saying you want to stay in this Sim… forever?"

"Absolutely… everything I want is right here… I have lots of friends… it's a good town, lot's to do… for fun…once you know the proper people… and IF you have some money."

"But I assumed you wanted to return to the real world?" I add.

"To me, Jim, this has become the real world… and I would prefer to stay right here… forever… if that is allowed."

Well, I certainly did not see that one coming. "I'm not sure… I see no logical reason why you can't stay here… I don't believe the game has an OFF switch… at least I never found one in the eleven years I was here."

"Good, then it's settled… now you and Jasmine accompany me up to my Penthouse suite… where I will serve you some excellent scotch, not the swill they serve down here… and later you can meet Gail."

I look over at Jasmine, "Let's us discuss this for a moment… if that is okay?"

"Sure… I have to go to the ladies room… so once I get back… just let me know."

Kathy leaves for the ladies room, and I look over at Jasmine, "Can you believe this… Kathy wants to stay in this Sim for the rest of her life… I am speechless…"

"Well, actually, Jim… it seems she has everything she was looking for… so why go anywhere else. You told me you programmed it to be as real as life itself, and that's why you named it *LifeSim*™."

"You have a point, I guess… but…"

"No buts… except… is that even feasible… what if someone eventually pulls the plug on the game? What happens to Kathy… and Gail?"

"Gail becomes vaporware, unfortunately, but Kathy should reset to her own *STR*… right where she left. I added that fail-safe feature just in case someone accidentally tripped over the *LifeSim*™ power cord while tens of thousands of folks are inside the game."

"I'll bet you did… probably trying to avoid a major lawsuit."

"Exactly."

"So what do we do, stay or go?" Jasmine asks.

"Well, since we have no specific time limit inside the *Sim*… and we will return to the exact *STR* we left 2048… we could stay for a while… just long enough to ensure Kathy is making a wise decision."

"And if we determine she is NOT making a wise decision, what then?"

"I suspect, in the end, it will be her decision to make."

"I agree… let's go meet Gail… and I do want to see this Penthouse suite you set her up in… and didn't even have sex with her?

"Yuk!" I respond.

"Yuk, what?" Kathy inquiries as she returns from the ladies room.

"Yuk to this sorry, Scotch," Jasmine covers, "Let's go to your suite and drink some of the good stuff."

"Now you are taking, and BTW, the drinks at the Bar are on me, since… well, apparently, I have a totally unlimited expense account."

Kathy and Gail

We use the executive elevator and we are in her suite in less than a minute. "OMG... this is fabulous... puts our poor suite to absolute shame," Jasmine offers once she's had the opportunity to snoop... er... observe the layout and facilities.

"Yea, Jim did well. And... honestly, Jim... a day never goes by that I do not thank you. When you came into my life I was miserable... poor... almost starving... and now I am one of the three richest folks in town."

"Third...? What...? Who are the other two...? I will have to look into taking some corrective action..." I state, obviously loving the attention.

"They are my friends... so leave them alone. We've started a few joint programs recently, to help the poor in town... there are others who are struggling, as I was."

"You mean... humans, not *Sims*?"

"Of course... *Sims* don't struggle..."

"There should not be other human's here?" I suggest, "That makes no sense."

"Apparently it does, Jim... and I now know why they are here... but first, let's get those drinks I promised... and within the hour, Gail will be joining us."

Kathy leaves for the Entertainment room... where the wet bar is located... of course. "How can someone live like this, Jim?" Jasmine offers, once Kathy is out of ear-shot.

"Exactly... no servants... she has to do everything herself... it's... uncivilized."

"You really are enjoying this, aren't you?" Jasmine offers.

"Yes, I am."

Kathy returns with the drinks, and some munchies. I take a bite of the cheese dip, "Well, some things haven't changed… still taste like wet cardboard."

"Yep, and that is on my short list of items you need to *fix* once you return to the 'real world'. I've gotten used to the bland food… but really… I am disappointed in you… you could do so much better."

I Look at Jasmine, "See… I told you Kathy was a *bitch*… a certified RB!" We all laugh at that off-hand remark (me, not so much).

We enjoy the 'good' scotch, and right on cue, Gail arrives. Kathy makes the introductions, and Gail joins us. Kathy gets up from her seat, "Gail is a wine drinker… hates scotch… so I'll be right back." She heads back to the wet-bar, and returns with what looks like a Merlot.

Gail takes a sip, "Excellent… thank you Kathy."

"No prob, love! Now, of course you know who Jim is… my savior… and Jasmine, apparently, is his love."

"Interesting," Gail states, "and you told me Jim was incapable of being loved." There is no smile (I told you Sims didn't have a sense of humor… maybe I need to work on that, too).

"Oh, he's not so awful… once you get to know him," Kathy responds.

I decide the pats on the back are over, so it is time to get down to the business at hand. "Gail, Jasmine and I came back to rescue Joyce from the Sim world she became trapped in… but, apparently, she does not want to be saved… she says she is happy right here."

"And why shouldn't she be? She has everything… and she has me… to love and to cherish for the rest of her life."

"So, you intend to spend the rest of your life with her?" Jasmine asks.

"Of, course, unless Kathy decides she no longer wants me… then, of course, I will leave."

I look at Kathy, but she makes no comments. "Kathy, what if, one day the money runs out… what would you do then?" I ask.

"That is not a problem, Jim, one of my financial well-to-do friends explained how everything works around here... and I have already begun to 'diversify my assets' across several categories... so, if tomorrow, my unlimited *Keycard* becomes... canceled... I will be fine. Of course, at first, I was concerned... once you dissolved out of existence... I panicked. But, after you left, I was still able to use my *Keycard*, and so, just as self-protection, I began diversifying... and in the last three months... I've set myself up to be self-sufficient."

"Good for you, Kathy," Jasmine offers.

"Anything else you need to know, Jim? I have made my decision, and while I do appreciate your concern for my welfare... I am a big girl... and can take care of myself."

"I see you can... and will not interfere with you staying in the Sim... for as long as it is active... but, you must understand, if the Sim ever goes away, you will be *Reset* back where you started... in 2054 I believe."

"Yes, I understand... but I expect you to keep the Sim alive... for me and the other Humans... and Sims who depend on it."

"I cannot promise that... but will try my best," I respond. "Okay, one more topic, and then Jasmine and I must go..."

"Sure."

"You said there were others... other humans... that you were trying to help."

"We are helping them!" Kathy responds, defensively.

"Yes, I'm sure you are... and you told me you knew why they were here... can you please explain?"

"Okay... but they need the same consideration that I'm getting... the right to make their own decision."

"Okay... I promise, but I need to meet them... and offer them a way back home."

"Fine! Here is what I've been told.... Most are political exiles... one of the owners of the *LifeSim*™ apparently has many political enemies... and if they ever cross him... he sends them here... for eternity... to repent for their sins against him."

"And what is the name of this person who ordered the exile?" I ask (as if I don't already know).

"Francis Jamison, do you know him?"

"Yes, he used to be my best friend and partner… but now… he is on my hit list… I can't wait to get back and deal with that ass-hole!"

"Priories, Jim," Jasmine states, and she is right. "Okay, when can I meet these human exiles… we need to do this sooner rather than later."

"Always… pushing… no wonder I never liked you…" Kathy responds, but she now gets the evil eye from Gail.

"Okay, fine… I will set it up… but it may take a couple of days… we met, periodically… and discuss… stuff… we distribute credits… and other items of necessity."

I have a bad feeling about this relationship, but decide not to go there. "I am certain you have improved their lot in life… but please, set up a meeting as soon as possible. I believe that Jasmine and I need to leave now… thanks for everything… we will be staying in the hotel, when you need to reach…"

"Absolutely not… you are staying here with us," Kathy replies. "We have five bedrooms… please stay here, Jim, Jasmine."

"Sure, no problem," I reply.

Safe Haven

Once we've eaten a proper dinner (local 'cardboard' style), we are shown to our rooms. Kathy leaves, and we close the door, "My God... she is a Royal Bitch if ever I've met one," Jasmine explains. "How did you put up with her, for what, a month?"

"I had forgotten how bad she really was... but none the less, Gail seems to like her... so... "

"Gail is a Sim... is she not programmed to like her?" Jasmine asks.

"It's not that simple, Jasmine, while *Sims* do not have free will, as such, they do have complex programming that allow them to make decisions... so if Gail likes Kathy... then there has to be a reason for that. So let's just drop this discussion... and concentrate on the other humans trapped here... at the hands of my ex-partner."

"Oh, BTW... I take it all back!" Jasmine states.

"Take what back?" I ask.

"You have my personal approval to kill that rat-bastard son-of-a-bitch at any time and in any method you deem appropriate... and all I ask is... that it not be a quick and painless death."

"I give you my promise... it will not be quick... and it will not be painless."

...

We do, eventually, sleep well, but neither of us is in the mood for sex... the situation is too intense... and we are unable to relax enough, but we do hold each other... and finally, sleep arrives.

Kathy provides a huge breakfast the next morning, a full buffet, and we have mimosas to drink. Gail is not with us, and I ask the obvious question.

"She sleeps here, but does have an assignment that she is required to fulfill. I see her most nights, and a couple of days ever week… it's the best we can do."

I decide not to inquire further, but drink my mimosa, relax and enjoy. Kathy goes out for a while, and returns in the early afternoon. Jasmine and I enjoy relaxing, socializing, and we even take a dip in the hotel pool.

"Well, I've set it up for tomorrow… 1PM. Everyone will be there… and so will a few of my friends."

I decide to ask no further questions, thank Kathy, and, Jasmine and I spend the rest of our day and evening alone, exploring the town. I have little more to say to Kathy. We get home late, are both in a much better mood, and make love for several hours.

I awake, it is after 11AM, and Jasmine is not here… so I rush, take a shower, and redress into my single set of clothes. I arrive in the entertainment room, and Jasmine is already there, having cocktails with Kathy. I join them.

"Ah, we were just talking about you, Jim," Kathy states, as she gets up and pours me a scotch. I want to tell her it is much too early for scotch… but why bother? It will probably just start another argument.

"So, where are we meeting these folks?" I ask… "And how many are there?"

"There are twelve, all told… but only ten are showing up… the other two, have already decided to stay… I informed them of the conditions and restrictions… and they agreed to them."

"Okay… where?" I repeat.

"Right here… they are all coming here… not to the suite, but down into conference room 107. I booked it for the afternoon."

"Okay, good."

"Jim, Jasmine and I have been talking… I really like Jasmine, BTW."

"Sorry, you don't like me as much… but I understand…"

"Do you?"

"No, I don't. What did I ever do to you to make you hate me so much?" I blurt out, un-expectantly.

"Not your fault, really. Basically you are a man... and I've had nothing but bad experiences with men... all my life... it started with my father... then my brothers... but I won't bore you with the details. My mom was weak... and I decided that I need to be strong in order to survive... so I became strong... self-sufficient..."

I have nothing to add to that commentary, so I decide, after all, to sip my scotch and remain quite.

...

At exactly 1PM, we head down to the conference room. There are only eight folks present. "Where are Gorge and Becky?" Kathy asks.

"They decided not to come... they will be staying," someone at the conference table decides to share.

"Okay, this is James Caldwell... inventor... creator and owner of *LifeSim*™," Kathy opens.

"Booooo... we hate you!"

"Ass-Hole..." I hear, as I take the floor, and look around at this... disheveled, and unhappy group.

I look over the room, and I understand. "I apologize for everything that has happened to you... but will not spend a great deal of time explaining it... since I really do not know the reason you are here... but I can take you all home... now... anytime you want. The nightmare is over... Jasmine and I are ready to leave here at any time... and any or all of you are welcome to join us."

"You are partners with the SOB... you are responsible..." one man shouts out.

"Yes, I am... and once we are all safely back home, I will make restitution to each of you... and your families... that I promise."

"What about Mr. Jamison," someone shouts.

"I will deal with him… harshly… my plan is to terminate his life."

"I hear a few 'oohs' but I continue. "He will pay for what he has done to you… you have my promise on that, as well."

"And how do you plan on doing that," someone else asks.

"Painfully… very painfully," I respond, "Any more questions before we go home?" I ask.

"And if we decide to stay here… what then?"

"I believe Kathy covered that… and that is your option… to stay or go… but we need to do this… now!" I state.

"When?"

"We leave in ten minutes… any objection?" I ask.

"Yes," an older man replies, "I have a family… I need to get them."

"Are they real or Sim?" I ask.

"Humans, of course… my entire family was brought here… we thought it was a vacation…"

"Sorry, but we have no time and I have no desire to hear individual horror stories… how much time do you need to get your family back here and ready for teleport?" I ask.

"At least an hour, but, I do want to thank you, Mr. Caldwell."

"For what?" I ask.

"For giving me that hundred credits, the first time we met… I never forgot that."

I look, and then I recognize him, the beggar, and I want to cry… but decide that any show of emotions or remorse will have to wait, "Anyone else need extra time?" I ask. No one speaks up, "So, we leave in an hour… go get your family."

I leave the conference room, head to the men's room, and begin to sob. I am depressed... how anyone could treat people this way… There will be a day of reckoning… and soon.

Jasmine is right behind me… "It will be okay, Jim… let's just get them home… it will be okay."

"Will it?" I respond.

…

I decide it is time to say goodbye to Kathy, "Are you certain this is what you want?" I ask.

"Yes, Jim, it is… I understand the risks… but even if I'm happy for just a few years… that is longer than I have ever been happy in my entire life."

"I am so sorry, Kathy."

"For what? You were wonderful to me. I understand what I did to you… but despite that… you gave me everything… I will never… ever forget you… thank you Jim."

Once again, I want to cry, but decide that now would be a good time to return to the conference room. As I enter, I see the family, a wife, and three children. "Are we all ready to leave?" I ask.

"Yes," they all state. Jasmine is next to me, I retrieve my *SmartComm*, and press *Return*.

Jasmine and I dissolve back into the _FgU_ lab, 2048. "Where are the others?" Jasmine asks.

"Oh, I sent them back to their original timelines. Their patterns were all on file in the Sim Host computer." I check my *SmartComm*… "All confirmed… they are home."

"What next?" Jasmine asks.

"We go home… back to 2350… we rest, and we plan the next rescue… and this one is going to be much more difficult… I assure you."

Part 4:
Sweet Revenge

Returning Home

Jasmine and I return to 2350… which I now consider as my home. We take several days… rest… and enjoy our first-round win.

"I must say, that was a stimulating… and inspirational adventure," Jasmine states.

"It was rewarding," I reply, "not sure about the other attributes… I am still a bit depressed."

"Why, every one returned home safely… and those who wanted to stay in the *Sim*…"

"Yes, but I worry about them. We are up here in 2350… and the *Sim* is back there in 2050… how can I possibly ensure their safety?"

"We will figure it out… You will figure it out. I now see the genius that I had overlooked before."

"Genius is easy to overlook… because all of the other crap that keeps getting in the way."

"So true," Jasmine responds.

...

It is a full week later that we begin our planning of phase 2, rescuing 'the girls from 1890 London'.

"Why do you always call them 'the girls'… that is such an outdated… and derogatory term to apply to grown women," Jasmine offers.

"I know it is… but it was Joyce who first called them that… and I guess the name just stuck."

"How about we lose it… right now?" she asks.

"You got it."

"So what is the plan?"

"Complicated… unless we find some way to simplify it. We need to go back before we found Brenda, dead and mutilated… that much is certain… and I'm thinking about going back even further for Joyce."

"Why not go back right after the three of you met, extract both ladies, and then return them to their timeline just like you did for the political prisoners and their families?"

"Well, that would certainly be the least traumatic for Brenda… but, that would not solve my problem with Joyce."

"Explain."

"By the time Brenda, Joyce and I got together… I was already madly in love with Joyce… and she with me. If I extract her at that point, I will have to explain *you*… and Joyce will be hurt."

"And you? Will you be hurt?"

"No, not if I am able to save them both… I can live with my loss of Joyce… do not worry about that for a minute," I reply, attempting to convince myself as well as Jasmine. For, in fact I did love Joyce… I do love Joyce.

"Okay, so what do we do?"

"First, we need to go back to the night of her death… extract Brenda, and then terminate 'Jack'. I'm not sure I can do anything about the one's he's already killed… but I can certainly stop him from killing again."

"How do you go about killing a *Sim*?" Jasmine asks.

"Oh, Jack the Ripper is not a *Sim*… he is quite real," I reply, with certainty.

"And how do you know that?"

"The game was quite controlled. Only monsters can kill… and that is usually confined to graveyards, castles, and other locations outside of the city itself… except at night when the zombies and vampires come calling."

"But you told me about that night you were almost killed… in the city."

"Yes, but that was a special circumstance… it was the *Bates Motel*, and anyone who choose to stay at that *Psycho* place…

knew what would be coming for them… that was actually in our sales and marketing brochures."

"Okay, so only monsters kill the players… can you be certain?"

"Yes… I programmed all of the monsters myself… and part of the control was that they could not look human… could not be confused with a human. You had to know they were coming after you… it had to be stated in your contract. Which is the reason the other humans I encounters never complained of monsters chasing them at night… they were not there to encounter monsters. I, on the other hand, unwisely choose to perform a 'Full Beta' which included all of the creatures, torture chambers… and other horrors that I, and others, had programmed into the game."

"So why were there no monsters when you and I went back?"

"Because we came in through a different portal… I selected the 'No monsters' option… when I downloaded the data from my *SmartComm*."

"You've thought of everything."

"No… unfortunately, I haven't. We had very little trouble on Phase 1… we might not be so lucky this time around."

"Not if you are planning on killing 'Jack'… that's for sure."

…

Based on what Jasmine and I discussed, I decide to give the plan a bit more thought before committing to any specific plan. But, finally it is time to commit to a plan. "Let's do this in two separate steps… or maybe three."

"Okay, I'm listening."

"Step 1… we go back, extract Brenda… and return her home."

"Any ramifications…? Will that complicate your timeline with Brenda and Joyce… put you into some sort of time dilemma… or paradox?"

"Good question, and *no*… I plan to extract her about a minute before 'Jack' shows up. Any earlier and he might be able to detect my presence and not show up at all… and later…"

"So you won't kill 'Jack' on the first trip?"

"No, that might put Brenda at risk… that is what the possible 3rd trip is for… but I'm still thinking through that part."

"I understand… then what?"

"Once Brenda is safety back in her timeline, then we must figure out the best time to rescue Joyce… and this is where a time paradox might arise…"

"Okay, so let's just do Phase 2a… and worry about 2b, 2c… afterwards."

"So it is decided. Phase 2a will extract Brenda, get her home, and return. Now, on second thought, you need to stay out of this one, Jasmine… what if I miscalculate and Jack shows up before I can send Brenda home?"

"Then don't let that happen… we've been over this… I will go back with you each time you return to the past… except for when you have to deal with your ex-partner. That decision is *not* up for re-discussion."

"Okay… just checking. Let's do this." I take Jasmine's hand, pull up the original program, press 'EXE'… and once it shows ready… I press 'Go'.

…

Once again, I look around… no *Me*, so I head to the *Sim* host master console, insert my *SmartComm*, download the new 1890 London *Sim* settings, and we head into the portal.

We rematerialize in my hotel suite, inside one of the unused bedrooms. Jasmine takes on the assignment of checking on Brenda, making sure she is okay. If Brenda sees Jasmine… she will be easier to explain then if Brenda sees me.

Jasmine creeps quietly out of the comfort of our current hiding place, and heads quickly towards Brenda's bedroom. She returns within several minutes, "She is asleep in her bedroom… let's go get here… now. You don't know exactly when Jack will show up… and I want to be long gone when that happens."

I nod, and we head back toward Brenda's bedroom… and we are almost at her bedroom door, when we hear the main door to the suite begin to creak… and slowly open. We are out of time… I grab Jasmine's hand, we run into Brenda's bedroom… and she awakes with a startle, "What the hell, Jim… and who is this?"

"No time… we have to go… take my hand… NOW!" I grab Brenda's hand but then realize I don't have a free hand to press the *Return* button. Jasmine realizes the situation at the exact same moment, drops my hand… reaches into my pocket, pulls out the *SmartComm*, but it drops to the floor.

"Fuck!" I hear her exclaim, as Jack pushes his way through the door… butcher knife in hand. For the first time, I get a good look at Jack… I will never forget that face… ever.

"What… oh… I get to take out all the players… at one time… how wonderful," He shouts, as he approaches me, large knife in hand, extended and ready to strike.

At least I am now certain Jack the Ripper is a real human, so I shout to Jasmine," Press the *Return* button… Now!" I jump Jack, and we both fall to the ground. I am hopeful of knocking the butcher knife out of his hand… but no such luck. As we hit the floor, he takes a swipe at me… and connects. I feel the pain in my left arm… but I've felt pain before… so this does not slow me down. I catch Jack by the throat, with both hands… and begin to squeeze… hard… just as I begin to feel the tingling… as we dematerialize out of 1890 and back into 2048.

More Drama

I am on the floor and Jasmine is standing above me, "Did Brenda get back home?" I ask.

"I assume so… no time for that… I've got to get you out of here… now… you are bleeding badly." Jasmine is still holding the *SmartComm*… and looking for the right button to push….

"What the fuck is going on?" I look up and there I am just entering the room, "Quick Jasmine… hit the master return… and let's get the…" and once again, I feel the tingle… and… we are home.

...

Apparently, I lose consciousness, but I awaken, and I'm in our bed… at home, and my arm hurts like hell. I am alone, "Jasmine!" I call.

She is there… "Welcome back to the living, my love… damn that was a close call… you lost a lot of blood… I had to get a porta-pack of generic, whole organic blood… and infuse you… I believe you will be okay. I am online to the Medics… they recommend bed rest, until the lost blood has had the opportunity to regenerate."

"Brenda… is okay?" I ask. My throat hurts, when I speak.

"Yes, your *SmartComm* confirmed she arrived back into 2054… that's all it said."

"Good…"

...

I awake and am looking at the ceiling, "Jasmine?" I ask, more quietly this time.

"I'm right here, Jim... the Medics want you to sit up and drink lots of fluids..."

"Good... I'll have a double scotch, rocks... my arm hurts like hell..."

"You wish... *drink*... as in water... lots of water..."

"Damn, I was afraid of that," I reply.

Jasmine hits the button, and the head of the bed rises to a comfortable position, and I drink water... lots of water... tons and tons of water... I believe I may drown. That does help my throat, but my left arm throbs. "Any drugs for the arm?" I ask, hopeful.

"No, all drugs are gone... we use only natural pain relievers here in this house."

"Damn, guess I should have stayed at the psych-ward... they had great drugs. Okay, as long as I can chase it with scotch... that will work."

"Now, Jim... okay... let's compromise... you can chase it with wine."

"My second choice."

...

It takes another full day before I am able to get out of bed, and move around. "Did my arm get infected?" I ask.

"It would have, but the blood contains antibiotics, and smart micro-Bots that assist with the healing process."

"Smart... *Bots*... not sure I want to know what they are... but I am feeling better."

"Good... are you up for questions... I have a few, regarding our last trip..." Jasmine states.

"Sure, fire when ready."

"First, despite the fact that you were hurt... I must confess that was the most exciting time... maybe of my entire life."

"Glad you enjoyed... must be dull up here in 2350."

"It's the price we pay for safety and stability... nothing exciting ever happens... so little drama... but I'm getting off point."

"And the point was?"

"That, despite you being hurt... it was a great adventure... I will never forget it... and I can't wait until the next one."

"Are you some sort of sadist?"

"Not sure what that words means... but... a little excitement is good for..."

"Don't tell me 'the heart'... I won't believe that."

"Okay, let's go with 'the soul' for now."

"Whatever floats your boat," I reply.

"So, what's next, Jim? Do we head back and rescue Joyce? Or do we, instead, go back and kill that rat-bastard, Jack?" Jasmine asks... obviously, raring to go.

"Right now... we rest... I need a small break from all of this fun and excitement."

Phase 2b

I decide that unless Jasmine asks specific questions about our last venture into the past... I will not volunteer any further information. It is too disturbing to deal with. What I saw was... sorry, I am at a loss for words...

...

It is less than a week later, when Jasmine finally asks, "Are we ready to plan our next rescue mission, Jim?" We are sitting in our living area, watching what, apparently, accounts for TV these days... something has definitely been lost over the last few hundred years.

"Yes, any time. And let me say this before we continue... I was wrong before... if you had not been there with me... then I would be dead... and so would Brenda... so thanks for your help."

"Oh, I would not have missed it for the world. And don't worry, I'm getting the hang of this time travel stuff... so if you had died... I would have come back and saved you... but you do need to teach me how to use the *Sim* host console... just in case."

"You got it... but we have to be cautious, the 2048 Jim has seen me twice... and since he is not the dullest tool in the shed... he may be suspecting... and that, in itself, could change the timeline. We must be more careful."

"Careful is my middle name," Jasmine responds.

"Yea... right. So... let's plan Phase 2b.... getting Joyce the hell out of there."

"Okay, so based on our prior discussions, we may need to go back a few weeks… to the point where you two had not yet fallen in love… and, just for the record… what exactly did you see in her?"

"We will not go there… moving on…"

"Okay, fine… be that way… but she and I will have a talk…"

"No, you will not!"

"We'll see… so when did you first know you loved her?" she asks.

"No, we are not going to revisit the past… just revise it. Let's go back to the first week Joyce and I met. There were a few times we were not together… let's pick one of those… based on the data stored in my *SmartComm*."

"So, is it true that Joyce was a prostitute… before you two met?"

"No, she was not a prostitute… but she did live on the streets because that is where they left her… for whatever reason."

"Okay, sorry."

"No you're not… you are, actually, gloating…"

"That was not a gloat… more of a… sigh of relief."

…

"Okay, so here is the plan," I begin, a few hours later, once we've both calmed down… through whatever means were available to us… at the time.

"I'm going to pick a time, in that first week, go back, tell her as little as I can… and then send her home. Since we have not yet fallen in love… then she will not be heartbroken… but just grateful for being able to get back home."

"And you?"

"We've already discussed this."

"Yea… but what happens once you see her again… and all of those emotions come back… what will you feel then?"

"Damn, Jasmine… you know I cannot predict that… who could. If *our* love is strong enough, then it will endure… if

230

not...? Are you sure you don't want to sit this one out... I should not need you..."

"No fucking way I'm leaving you alone with... that woman... for a single second."

"Okay... then let's do this."

We stand, hold hands, I start the program, and Press Go.

...

He is waiting for us... rather, I am waiting for us...

"I thought you two would be back... so let's just stop... all take a deep breathe... and you can tell me what the fuck is going on. Are you my clone?" I ask myself, as he takes hold of my arm and we head over to a small table.

We take a seat, and actually, he... I serves wine... how civilized is this. "I assumed you would want something to calm you nerves... and I know just the thing."

"Okay, to answer your first question... I am not your clone... you are mine... It was a diabolical scheme set up twenty years ago..."

"Bull-shit... now, don't try to be funny... you were NEVER funny."

"And neither were you, I bet," Jasmine adds.

"And who is this... your psychic friend from the future?"

"She's my psychic... and my lover... this is Jasmine...and she already knows who you are."

"Nice to meet you, Jasmine... I have never seen hair quite that color before... you must be from the future."

"Gee," I reply. "And how could you have guessed... you must be intuitive."

"Maybe... but..."

"No buts... now shut up and listen to me," I state. "We *are* from the future, but if we tell you anything... anything... it could change the timeline going forward... and we cannot have that... not now."

"Why? What timeline... is something wrong?"

"Nothing you need to be concerned with. You need to proceed on your current course... and not vary... based on anything we say here... understood?" I state, emphatically.

"I am not liking this... one damn bit." He... I respond.

"It is the safest course of action. We are leaving now... we are heading through that portal... and you will not stop us... you will not interfere... and you will try your best to forget you ever met us."

"I doubt I can do that," I reply to my statement.

"Then drink lots of scotch... and try to forget."

"I don't drink scotch," I reply.

"You will... we must go." Jasmine and I get up from the table and head to the master console. "Take the *SmartComm*, and insert it into that slot, and then press the 'EXE' button down here." Jasmine does as I ask... and several options display on the screen in front of us. "Select Download pre-selected data."

She does so, and the console flashes green. "Now let's head into the portal... there is a ten second delay before the program executes and we are transferred into the Sim."

I retrieve my *SmartComm* and we head into the portal...

We are back in 1890 London. We are walking down the main street of London, "Heads up, we will see them shortly... and if memory serves and my *SmartComm* is accurate, they will separate right here... Joyce will head into that store, and I will head to the pub next door to wait on her."

We watch for another two minutes, and Jasmine spots them walking down the street... not holding hands. They stop, look at each other, and Joyce heads into the store, while I (old I) heads next door into the pub.

"I'm going into the store to talk with Joyce... you coming?" I ask.

"No, I think I'll head in and have a chat with you... Jim... old you..."

"Don't you fuck this up, Jasmine... if he learns anything... it could change the timeline from this point forward."

"I know... I just want to meet you back here in 1890... I promise not to do anything... bad." We part company, and I head into the store, directly behind Joyce. She is looking at ladies' dresses, when I arrive.

She looks up, sees me, and smiles, "Oh, I thought you were going next door to the bar... wait... you look different... your hair is shorter... your outfit... what the fuck?"

"Please, let's walk over here and walk," I tell her, as I hold out my hand. We head over and take two seats right outside the dressing room. "Now listen, Joyce. I told you I would make every attempt to get you out of this *Sim* and back home... right."

"Yes, but..."

"No, listen. I have come back from the future... I did get out... and now I've come to take you back home."

"Now?"

"Yes, right now... you will arrive exactly where you left... except a few months later... Go home and have a wonderful life. Do not, under any circumstances, ever go back to _FgU_ ... do you understand?"

"Yes... but I have questions..."

"I'm sorry, but there is no time for questions... you are leaving now." I take out my *SmartComm*, press 'Single Return', and Joyce dissolves out of existence... and my life. I, however, continue to sit in the chair and look... where she was... just a few moments ago. My God, I realize... I loved that woman... and part of me wants to go back to 2054... and be with her.

I am still staring at the empty chair, when I feel Jasmine take my hand, "Did you send her back?"

"Yes, she is home."

"Good... then let's leave, now."

I nod, and press the "Return all" icon.

My Loss

We are back home, and I am immediately thrown into the depths of depression. Jasmine seems to get it, and provides me the space I need to heal. We talk very little our first few hours back in 2350, I sip my wine and Jasmine reads one of her books.

I am finally ready to discuss… "The trip was successful, Joyce is back home… and hopefully, the timeline has not been disturbed."

"Yes, that is good… but I am sorry for your loss."

"What do you mean? The trip was successful… there was no loss."

"Yes, there was… I now understand how much Joyce meant to you."

"How?"

"I followed you into that bar…sat next to you, and we talked… It was obvious how much you already loved her… I could see it in your eyes, when you discussed her."

"Thanks, Jasmine… for understanding."

"Did you make the right decision… choice?" she asks, almost at a whisper.

I take Jasmine's hand and look her directly into both eyes, "Absolutely… I made the right choice… I love you, Jasmine."

...

"Is there anything you can do about the girls who are still out there… in 1890?" Jasmine asks, several days later.

"Not certain about the dead ones, but yes, if I am able to stop Jack on the night he attempts to kill Brenda… then at least they will be alive… and maybe I will eventually find a way to retrieve them via the *Sims* master console."

"I didn't know that was possible?" Jasmine replies.

"I'm not at all sure it is… I certainly did not program an individual retrieval program… although maybe I should have."

"So what is your plan? Based on your last encounter with Jack… he almost killed you… he is much larger… stronger… than you."

"Yes… but now that I know who he is… that should give me a slight advantage.' I reply.

"What? You know him? But how could you?"

"Jack the Ripper is my old partner…. Francis Jamison!"

"You are fucking kidding me!"

"Oh, yes, and was I ever surprised. Not only is this ass-hole responsible for sending his political enemies into the *Sim*… never to be seen again, but he goes back there… and kills the females he sent into the game… and I need to know why he does that!"

"No, you do not… you need to stop him from killing those women… take him out of the game… figuratively and literally!" Jasmine states, and she is up in my face.

"Yes, I know… but why is he doing this?"

"Why do psychopaths ever kill anyone…? They get some sort of morbid satisfaction out of the chase… the capture, and the kill. Fuck that, Jim… find this freak… and terminate him!"

"I thought you were opposed to me killing him?"

"No… that was before… this is after. And the only thing I would suggest is, and I've told you this before… if you have a choice between a slow and painful, or a quick and painless one… please pick the slow and painful death!"

"No promises."

The Final Mission

"Okay, here is what I am thinking," I begin, once Jasmine has backed away and calmed down a little. "I will not go back and confront Jack, but instead, I will go back and deal with Francis... and kill two birds with one stone."

"I never cared much for that old saying... until now," Jasmine offers. "But, I am coming with you... I must watch this happen..."

"Absolutely not! This is one thing I *will do* on my own. This will not be easy... and I must do this all myself."

"No way... we agreed..."

"No, we agreed to do everything together up to this point, but my ex-partner is mine... all mine." I am now up in Jasmine's face... it is such a beautiful face, so I kiss her cheek and back away."I must do this, Jasmine... he was my partner... he betrayed me... he has murdered folks... and sent others into exile."

"I have a bad feeling about this, Jim... please let me help you?"

"Be waiting for me upon my return... that is what I want... what I need you to do."

"Okay, but I want you to return to this exact *STR*... do you understand. I will give you five minutes, and if you are not back... I will come back for you."

"Okay... agreed. If I am not back in 5 minutes... come get me." We touch *Comms*, and Jasmine downloads all of my data to her *P*Comm.

"Good luck, sweetheart... remember... I love you!"

"And I love you... hang in... be back in a moment."

...

I decide to confront my ex-partner right after he had me declared dead in 2058. He should no longer be on the defensive... it will be a lot less complicated getting him where I want him... and take him out of this game, forever.

Based on Jasmine's request, I program my *SmartComm* for a return to current *STR* one minute after I leave. "What weapons do you have?" Jasmine asks.

"Weapons... I have no weapons... just my god-given brain," I respond, as I press the 'EXE' button and fade out of 2350 and into 2058.

...

I arrive in the lab... but in one of the many storage facilities we have on premises. Since I left in 2049... and this is 2058... then I am just guessing as to Francis' exact location. If this doesn't work out, I can always hit the trusty return button... re-plan, and do this again on another day.

I exit the storage facility and head for Francis' office, assuming he has not moved. Once you are inside *FgU*, there is little or no security... the hard part is getting into the building. I chose to arrive at this exact time, 10:00AM, since he was a creature of habit, and was always in his office and setting up his daily log at that exact time. I arrive on the 14th floor, and casually walk out of the elevator. Thankfully, I spot on one that I recognize... it's been ten years since I've left... let's just hope my luck holds out. As I turn the corner, I see Francis' oversized office up ahead. I scan from left to right... but spot no one in any of the offices... that is strange... usually, this time of day...

I see Francis, head down, working on his schedule... or something to that effect. I decided to confront him here at the office, in broad daylight, for one simple reason; with everyone around, he would not dare attempt to kill me. I don't expect him to voluntarily turn himself in but once I get him on video... confessing to his crimes... then I will turn that evidence over to the police... and let them handle his arrest. I know... I said I would kill him, but it comes down to this... I am simply not a killer... for any reason.

I walk quickly, but quietly toward his office, the door is cracked, but almost closed, and he still has not seen me. There are windows on each side of the door... but since it is a wooden door, I head toward the center of the door, out of his line of sight. I arrive... I hear him typing on his keyboard... I take a deep breath, kick the door fully open... and I am starring into the barrel of what appears to be a 9mm pistol.

"You dumb ass son-of-a-bitch," Francis states as he stands, and points the pistol at my head, "I knew you would be here... not on this exact day... but at this time... and I've been waiting for you. Come in, please... have a seat."

"You won't kill me... the gunshot will bring others... you will be charged with murder... and since it will be a planned murder... you'll get the needle, for sure," I respond, with my best fully-confident sarcastic smile exposed. "Now put the gun down... and we can talk... partner... friend."

"Ass-hole, loser," he replies. "And boy, are you dumb!" Once again, you underestimated me... and for the last time. There is no one here to witness me murdering you. After I had you declared dead last month... I fired everyone in the company... they are all gone... no one here but us maniacs."

"Why?" I ask, as I slowly take a seat... as far away from the barrel of the gun as I can get.

"Because I didn't need *FgU* anymore... all I needed was your three billion credits... and, once I had you declared dead... and produced the forged will... what did I need a company for? And, just as soon as you are really dead... chopped into extremely small pieces, and disposed of, I will sell the building. You are such a fool!"

"Yes, I guess I am... and a trusted one at that... why did you do it, Francis? Once we get the game started... you would have made billions... legitimately... so why sabotage... I don't understand that part, at all."

"I know you are recording this entire conversation… but no matter, once I chop you into tiny pieces… I will take care of your recorder."

"You still have not answered my question… why?"

"Because I knew your silly game would fail… we would end up in bankruptcy… I never believed in it for a second… so, I decided to use it to my own advantage… to take care of all of those people who, over the years, betrayed me… kept me down… and for all those women who I tried to love… but refused to love me back. Oh, yea, you met one of those… Brenda… And you think you saved her from me… ha. Any other burning questions before you die?"

"So, really, you are just a pathological killer, after all?"

"Call me whatever you wish… I have your money… and once you are dead… I will have my revenge."

"Revenge for what, Francis? What did I ever do to you? We have been friends since middle school… and we were partners… what makes you hate me so much?"

"Oh, that is an easy one… and unfortunately… your last question. All your life, you've had the silver spoon in your mouth… everything came easy to you... you just looked at it, batted your cute blue eyes, and it turned to gold. I worked hard for years… and what did it get me…? No woman loved me… I made a little money… but nothing like you… so I decided to have it all… and your fucking *Sim* game gave me the means and opportunity to get everything I wanted… needed. Once I sent you into the *Sim*… on a one-way trip, I decided to deal with the others in my life who had dared to fuck with me. You were able to get a few out, I am guessing… but there are hundreds of others in there… scattered across time and space. Sorry, but speaking of time… your time is up. I've got a messy job ahead of me… and so I had better get to it."

I see a glimmer behind Francis, and take the opportunity to dive behind his desk, I hear two shots, and I roll out the other side, spring forward… but it is already too late.

As I return to my feet, I see Jasmine, large machete in hand, swinging at Francis' head. I want to shout… no… but I watch, as in slow motion, the machete slices through his neck, severs

239

his head completely... and I watch as his head slowly descends toward the floor... where it bounces, once... spewing blood everywhere.

I look over at Jasmine... she drops the machete, points her *P*Comm at me... and we dissolve back into 2350.

Rectify Past Sins

We've been back home a week, and Jasmine is beginning to return to some semblance of normality. She was in shock for a few days, cried for a couple more, and then went into depression. I was there for her every minute of every day. I decided never to discuss this again. If the time comes when Jasmine needs to talk about it… we will… but what can I really say? I would be dead, now, had it not been for Jasmine. I will never forget that… and there are many other things I will never forget. The nightmares have already started, and I suspect they will continue for a long while.

...

I decided I must make one more trip back to the past. I will plan it myself… Jasmine will not be involved… she has done quite enough. Of course, she goes to counseling every day, and that too, will continue for quite a while… maybe forever. I decide to head back to 2048… meet myself and tell him everything that has gone down. I fully realize this creates a paradox… but I need his help.

...

I arrive, and he is waiting for me… sitting in a chair, with two glasses of wine in hand. "I knew you'd be back… you are so predictable," he states.

Once I explain the purpose of my trip, Jim (2048) is all in. "I never really trusted Francis, Jim," he states.

"Bull-shit, Jim… I trusted him… you trusted him… let's not go there. I have a plan… let's discuss it, agree to it… and then execute it."

Our plan is two-fold. First, we need to identify and then rescue all of the people Francis sent into exile in my *Sim* Game. We cannot do that from 2048, so we both head to 2058… right after Francis' death. Jim (2048) takes the lead on this mission… goes to the Police, and tells them essentially what has happened. He, of course, knows nothing about his partner's death… and is quickly absolved of that crime. Next, he goes to court to get back control over both the three billion credit assets and the *Sim* Game. That takes a few months to accomplish.

Once the legal aspect of this fiasco had been resolved, we returned to 2048… and begin the process of retrieving the folks from the *Sims*. Francis was adamant about logging his details, and even though they were highly encoded, we were able, eventually, to uniquely identify all of the individuals he sent into exile and in which *Sim STR* they were imprisoned.

Slowly… one or two at a time, Jim (2048) and I head into the *Sim*, retrieve the folks, and send them back home. This takes over a month to accomplish. Unfortunately, we do not find them all. In the end, over a dozen folks remain unaccounted for. Hopefully, they are alive and happy in one of our *Sim* worlds.

As for Brenda, based on what my ex-partner told me during our last meeting… we have to go forward in time and locate her. It takes a while, but finally we succeed. She is dead. Head chopped off… and the killer was never located.

We make the only decision available to us… we go back in time, extract her shortly before her death, and move her forward to after the time Francis was killed. She loses five years of her life… but does get to keep that life.

…

I want to go forward and visit Joyce… see how she is doing… but decide that is not feasible. I have another brilliant idea… but it will need to wait. We have one more task to accomplish.

"So how can we ensure the *Sim* continues to operate... for years to come, so that those folks who decided to stay... like Kathy, and others... can have a full and complete life?" I ask Jim (2048).

"Simple, I will head back to 2058, and since I own the rights to the game, I will set up a sort of trust... pay forward a hundred years and then seal the game completely... ensuring that no one can ever tamper with any of the *Sims*... and they will continue to operate."

"Don't forget the battery backup," I recommend. Jim (2048) does not smile... he was so un-cool back then... no sense of humor...

...

It is now time to say goodbye to Jim (2048) and return to Jasmine. Of course, I will arrive five minutes after I left... and will continue to help Jasmine recover... from the extreme trauma she has suffered... on my behalf.

I decide that now is the time... to resolve that final dilemma. "Jim, ole buddy... I need you to do one last little thing for me," I state.

"I have already done dozens of things for your... saved your ass... saved you ass... did I mention the times I saved your ass?"

"I believe you did, and BTW, that was your own ass you saved... so don't expect a box of candy on Valentine's Day."

"Okay... what do I need to do to get you to leave? You have definitely worn out your welcome."

"I am hurt. Okay, here it is. We have a love... that you have not yet met... trust me, she is the love of your life. I have her space-time coordinates and you need to go forward... find her and..."

"And, what?"

"Oh, you will know, my brother, once you meet Joyce. She is everything a man could want...and if you promise to do this for me... I will head back to the future, to be with my love... Jasmine."

"And if I decide not to do this… task for you?"

"Oh, trust me… I will come back and haunt you… over… and over… until the day you die."

"Is she that special?"

"Oh yes, she is that special."

"Then I promise to do this… if you will promise to get the fuck out of 2048… and never come back."

"I promise."

Epilogue

It takes a while, but Jasmine finally comes back to me. She killed another human being... a monster, but a human none-the-less, and that act will haunt her for the remainder of her life. We are very happy in 2350... and I have no intentions to ever returning to the past. Those days are over. I will live in the present... in the *Now*, for the rest of my hopefully long and happy life with Jasmine.

"So, Jim," Jasmine begins, after we've had our morning coffee, "What shall we do today?"

"Whatever your little heart desires, my dear," I respond as I take hold of her hand.

"Well, you said you would like to visit some of the other *SkyCities*... we haven't done that... how does that sound?"

"Perfect, I would love that, but in your condition... should we be traveling?" I ask.

"Sure, the medics say that I can travel up to the seventh month... where shall we go?"

"Anywhere you want?" I respond.

"Okay... then let's go to SC: New Orleans... I've always wanted to visit that *SkyCity*."

"Sounds like a plan. Now remind me again... how do we get over there?"

"Oh that's easy... we just take the *Caldwell Teleporter*... and once we arrive..."

The End

CPSIA information can be obtained
at www.ICGtesting.com
Printed in the USA
BVHW070827311218
536775BV00036B/1552/P